PENGUIN CRIME FICTION

BRANDSTETTER AND OTHERS

Joseph Hansen was born in South Dakota
in 1923 and as a young boy moved to South-
ern California, where he has lived ever
since. Now settled in Los Angeles with his
wife, Jane, and a household of cats and
dogs, he teaches mystery writing for UCLA
Extension. He is the author of seven popular Dave Brandstetter mysteries and several
others, including *Backtrack* (also published
by Penguin), which he is currently adapting
for the stage with playwright Arch Brown.

Brandstetter & Others

Five Fictions by
JOSEPH HANSEN

PENGUIN BOOKS

PENGUIN BOOKS
Viking Penguin Inc., 40 West 23rd Street,
New York, New York 10010, U.S.A.
Penguin Books Ltd, Harmondsworth,
Middlesex, England
Penguin Books Australia Ltd, Ringwood, Victoria, Australia
Penguin Books Canada Limited, 2801 John Street,
Markham, Ontario, Canada L3R 1B4
Penguin Books (N.Z.) Ltd, 182–190 Wairau Road,
Auckland 10, New Zealand

First published in the United States of America by
The Countryman Press 1984
Published in Penguin Books 1986

LIBRARY OF CONGRESS CATALOGING IN PUBLICATION DATA
Hansen, Joseph, 1923–
Brandstetter & others.
Reprint. Originally published: Woodstock, Vt.:
Countryman Press, 1984.
Contents: Election day—The Anderson boy—The
tango bear—Surf—[etc.]
1. Detective and mystery stories, American.   2. California—Fiction.
I. Title.   II. Title:
Brandstetter and others.
[PS3558.A513B7   1986]   813'.54   85-31083
ISBN 0 14 00.7738 3

These stories first appeared as follows, and are reprinted with permission:

"Election Day," *Ellery Queen Mystery Magazine*, November 1984
"The Anderson Boy," *Ellery Queen Mystery Magazine*, September 1983
"The Tango Bear," *Ellery Queen Mystery Magazine*, December 1984
"Surf," *Playguy* (London), January 1976
"Willow's Money" is published here for the first time.

Printed in the United States of America by
George Banta Co., Inc., Harrisonburg, Virginia
Set in Baskerville

for Lou Kannenstine & Peter Jennison

Contents

Brandstetter & Others

Election Day

Shabby brick store-fronts slept against a background of brown hills in October sunlight that hadn't yet warmed up. It was early, but a place that served breakfast ought to be awake. Dave looked for it. This drab east end of Hollywood rarely saw much traffic. Now it consisted of a single faded peewee pickup truck, inching its way along at the curb, a mohawk-haired college age boy in sweat pants and tank top trotting beside it. When the truck paused, he reached into it for a poster, red with white lettering. He slapped the poster against the naked trunk of a soaring palm tree and, with a shiny gun, stapled the poster in place. CATTON FOR CONGRESS. He and the truck moved on.

FAMOUS FARMHOUSE BREAKFASTS had a snappy new sign, and an artfully antiqued plank front covering the original brick. A width of inky new blacktop beside it was painted with white bias lines. Dave left his Jaguar there and tried the knob of a door under a little outcrop of shingled roof. The knob turned but the door didn't give. He blinkered his eyes with cupped hands and peered through the glass. No one sat on counter stools nor at the small tables surfaced with gingham patterned Formica. Behind the counter, glass coffee pots gleamed empty. Through a wide service window sheltered by another shingled roof edge, Dave saw no one moving in the kitchen. Things looked a little dusty.

He frowned at his watch. Seven thirty-two. *Open daily, 6:00 A.M. till 2:00 P.M.* was crisply lettered on the door glass. But CLOSED, a cardboard sign said, *Sorry We Missed You.* Dave glanced up and down the street. No one headed on foot for Famous Farmhouse Breakfasts. Only one car was in sight, parked up the block on the other side. Had Harvey and Carolyn Sweetzer given up? If so, where were they? They weren't at home. He'd been to their boxy stucco tract house before the dew had evaporated from the composition roof. No one had answered his ring at the front door nor his knock at the back. No car had stood in the driveway, none in the garage. He had misjudged the time they left for work. But they plainly weren't at work. So where were they? Carolyn Sweetzer's sister Elizabeth was dead, but they wouldn't be at a mortuary—not this early.

He sighed. His practice of not telephoning ahead sometimes wasted time in this way. He liked face-to-face encounters. People's expressions, the look in their eyes, the way they fidgeted if they did, or stiffened if they did, often told him what words wouldn't on the phone. The element of surprise sometimes made people blurt things out before they'd had a chance to think. He turned away. He'd gauged locating the Sweetzers to be a sure bet. Little businesses like this held people close. He'd been wrong, hadn't he? There were no sure bets. He was dropping into the leather seat of the Jaguar when a car caromed into the parking lot and squealed to a sharp stop. A thin, balding man jumped out of it. He wore a beige polyester suit.

"Harvey Sweetzer?" he said.

"Sorry," Dave said. He had seen the man before, at the marshal's, at the court house. He was a process server. Carmichael? Some name like that. "What's wrong?"

Carmichael had reached into the inside pocket of his jacket and half drawn out a paper. His face fell, and he pushed the paper back out of sight. "I know you," he said. "Damn, I thought I was getting a break." He frowned, chewed a thin, pale lower lip, then brightened. "Insurance, right? Death claims? Wait, I got the name to go with it. Brandstetter." Dave nodded, and shook the cool, lifeless hand the man offered. The man's smile faded. "Oh, no. You don't mean to tell me he's dead. Oh, boy—is that going to leave a lot of people hung out to dry."

"Creditors?" Dave said.

"All that remodelling." The man waved a thin arm. "Outside, inside. Stoves, refrigerators, ventilation—you know what restaurant equipment costs? Contractors, painters, electricians, plumbers. He was crazy. Everybody who gave him credit was crazy." He waved at the street. "Look at this neighborhood. Who do you see? Nobody. Three months ago, six, maybe, yeah. There was a plant where they assembled ballpoint pens, all right? Fifty, sixty workers. There was a lens-grinding lab, you know? Eyeglasses? Say another couple dozen people. But they folded. I mean, the country is in the worst shape since the Depression, so Harvey Sweetzer goes in hock twenty thousand bucks to fix up a broken down beanery. What did it do—dawn on him? Did he kill himself? Is that why you're here?"

"It's about Bess Jessup," Dave said.

"The one that used to be a singer?" Carmichael nodded, sunlight glaring off his scalp. "Murdered. I saw it on the TV news. What's she got to do with Sweetzer?"

"She was his sister-in-law," Dave said.

Carmichael drew breath for another question, then didn't ask it. He turned his head a little, regarded Dave from the corners of his eyes, frowning. He gave a soft whistle. "Oh, hey. I get it. She had a life insurance policy, right? And it just so happens Harvey Sweetzer is the beneficiary?"

Dave pulled his legs into the Jaguar, closed the door, ran the window down. "Could be," he said, and started the engine. He smiled. "You could get your money, yet. Can I ask you to move your car?"

"Yeah, sure. I got a lot of other suckers to hunt for." Carmichael got into his no-color, no-model car. "Two things there's no shortage of." He slammed the door. "Optimism and bad debts." He backed the car into the empty street.

The fair-haired, blue-eyed boy in orange jail coveralls said, "He knocked, and it was a code knock she knew from before. She whispered to be quiet and he'd go away. But he knew she was there. And in a minute, he was tramping through the place, yelling her name. The bedroom door slams open, and he calls her bitch, drags her out of the bed, and starts punching her out."

Rader was the boy's name, and he sat looking glum, on a gray-green steel chair, forearms resting on a gray-green steel table. Dave had seen his record. Rader had worn jail coveralls before. He still looked as if he should be rehearsing the role of an angel in a Christmas pageant. The man who looked as if he belonged in jail coveralls stood behind Rader, leaning against a gray-green wall, hands pocketed. Squat, swarthy, low-browed, Bren Larkin was a public defender. His tough appearance always amused Dave. The man was a model of decency.

Dave sat opposite Rader. He reached behind him and probed the pockets of the blue denim jacket he'd hung on the back of his chair. He brought out cigarettes, and pushed the pack across the table. Rader took a cigarette. Dave lit it for him. Rader said, "What kind of watch is that?"

Dave put away the lighter. "Matthiesen," he said. "So you jumped him with your knife."

"Which you were not supposed to have," Larkin said, "under the conditions of your parole."

"The conditions are stupid," Rader said. "This is Los Angeles, not Sweetwater. In Los Angeles, big, black pimps come charging in on you when you're doing it with your girl." He looked through cigarette smoke at Dave. "The knife was in my jeans. On the floor. I yelled at him to cool it. Hell, he didn't even look my way. So I dove and got the knife and ran at him. He got the knife away from me and I got cut, didn't I?" He rubbed his ribs, wincing. "Bess was passing out, I was spouting blood, okay? Nothing happened to him. But he was the one who ran."

"No one saw him," Larkin said, "come or go. You ran, though. Stancliff saw you. The landlord."

"Hats Jimmerson was there." Rader looked sullen and stubborn. "I can't help it if the landlord didn't see him. Damn right I ran. It was my knife, wasn't it, and I wasn't supposed to have it, and I wasn't supposed to be consorting with ex-convicts and criminals, and I wasn't supposed to get in fights. The landlord was coming. 'What's happening? What's the matter?' I grabbed my clothes and went out the bedroom window and down the alley."

"Forgetting the five thousand dollars?" Larkin said.

"I never heard of a Matthiesen watch," Rader said. "It looks expensive."

"It isn't," Dave said. "Not very."

"There wasn't any five thousand dollars," Rader said.

Larkin said, "In a brown supermarket sack."

"Give up." Rader looked disgust over his shoulder. "The detectives said it was wrapped in white plastic." He looked at Dave with a thin, pitying smile. "They're all alike. Think everybody's as stupid as they are. He wants me to say, 'No, it was wrapped in newspapers,' right?"

"He's on your side," Dave said.

"Nobody's on my side." Rader reached for a Pepsi can on the table. The bright chains on his wrists rattled. He tapped ash off his cigarette into the small opening in the top of the can. "I didn't see any five thousand dollars in any sack or plastic or newspapers or anything."

"It was there when they found her dead that night."

"She was alive when I left her," Rader said.

"It was your knife that killed her," Larkin said.

"Last I saw it, Hats had it," Rader said, "staring at it like it scared him shitless. My blood all over it. He must have dropped it before he ran out." Rader dragged on the cigarette and coughed. "Look, even the cops admit my fingerprints aren't on the knife."

"Only Bess Jessup's," Larkin said. "But it was your knife, you had a loud argument with your girl, you beat her up—the bruises are there to show it. The landlord heard the fight and saw you run. You have a record of robbery with violence. You used to beat up your wife when you had one."

Rader nodded. He looked thoughtfully at the manacles on his wrists. He slowly moved his wrists apart, stretching the chain, as if measuring it for something. "If she'd had five thousand dollars," he said, "she would have told me about it. She'd have been wild with excitement. She'd been trying every which way to raise money for that record deal. She didn't say anything."

"Maybe she knew you the way the police know you," Larkin said. "Maybe she was afraid you'd steal it."

Rader smiled wryly at Dave. "And he's on my side?"

"He's thinking the way the D.A. would think," Dave said.

"Bullshit," Rader said. "I didn't take the money. It was there. You call that thinking?" He twisted his head to look at Larkin again. "Make sense, will you? Was it hidden—the five thou? Wasn't it out in plain sight? Didn't somebody say it was laying on the coffee table with her guitar?"

"That's where it was," Dave said.

"That doesn't mean she didn't have it in a closet," Larkin said, "and you found it, and she came in from the store or something and caught you taking it, and that was when the fight started, and you killed her."

"And then went off without the money?"

"You panicked. The landlord was banging on the door."

"I panicked, but I remembered to wipe my prints off the knife? Shit." Rader poked his cigarette into the Pepsi can, and stood up. "I want to go back to my cell. And I want another lawyer. Why didn't I take the knife with me?"

"Why didn't Jimmerson bring her the five thousand?"

"She was scared of him, she was hiding from him, for Christ sake. Ask him for money? He'd have her peddling her ass in bars again. He'd have her back on heroin. She was through with that life. She was going back to her singing career. She was good, you know? Beautiful. Listen to her tapes. She hadn't touched a twelve-string in years, but she was getting it all back. She was really working at it."

"Maybe Jimmerson killed her," Larkin said. "Finding her in bed with you. Before she went to prison for dealing, she was his lady. Maybe you're covering for him because if you don't, he'll kill you too. He cut you to warn you."

Rader shook his head. "She was alive when I left."

"Yup." Larkin sighed, pushed away from the wall, rapped thick knuckles on the interrogation room door. "I wish to hell she'd called the police."

"She didn't want me going back to Q," Rader said.

A uniformed officer opened the door from the hall.

Stancliff walked from his door down a long white room with skylights to a big broad drafting table, where he picked up a white mug with "S" on it. He slurped coffee from the mug and raised inquiring brows at Dave. "Coffee?"

"No thanks." Dave looked at the drafting table. Cut-up sheets of printed matter on high gloss paper lay there. Photographs. Miscellaneous letters of the alphabet in various type sizes and faces. Steel rulers, triangles, T-squares, French curves in thick amber plastic. X-acto knives and blue pencils. "Her place isn't sealed any longer. What have you done with her possessions?"

"Nothing. I only straightened up the worst of the mess." Stancliff set down the mug and perched on a stool at the table. "Stuff was thrown every which way. Drawers, clothes, couch cushions. Otherwise, it's the way I found it." He was an attenuated man, with a trimmed gray beard, gray hair over his ears, horn rim glasses. Cheap white cotton gloves covered his bony hands. "Fall is my busy season. Usually it's only Christmas—advertizing fliers, all that. But this year it's elections, too. All I do is work and sleep." His laugh was wry. "And not really all that much of the latter." He pushed papers around, looking for something. "It will be January before I get down there." He found a brush with long, soft bristles, and gently ran these over a pristine sheet of tagboard. He began to rule the tagboard with blue lines and corners, frowning, careful but quick.

Dave walked into a kitchenette at the far end of the room. Breakfast dishes were in the sink. There were vague smells of bacon and toast. A window was over the sink. He looked out and down. Below were garages, a small patio with floppy green plants in corners, a redwood gate to an alley. "I'd like a look at the place," he said.

"Here's the key." Stancliff rummaged among push-pins, ruling pens, erasers, in a gray metal fishing-tackle box. "She didn't have much. She'd just come out of a drug rehab program, you know. Clothes, guitar, tape recorder, and a carton of old clippings—that was about it. Everything else came with the apartment." He laid a key in Dave's hand.

"Thank you." Dave went down the long room again. Books were stacked everywhere. Art magazines. On a roughly-built plank loft in a corner lay a mattress with tumbled blankets. On the ladder to the loft cast-off clothes hung—none of them women's clothes. Dave stopped at the door. "She was right down below you. A musician. Trying to write new songs, take up a career again. Wasn't it noisy?"

"Nothing distracts me when I'm working. Concentration. That's the secret of success. Look around you. Conspicuous, isn't it—my tremendous success in life?" He drew another blue line. "Only the fights. They bothered me."

"You mean with Mike Rader? Had he beaten her before?"

"Not that. Just arguments. She was high-strung, lost her temper easily. He didn't know how to handle it. Sometimes I wondered if I'd been wise, renting to her. I didn't like that kid. What did she want with him, anyway? He was young enough to be her son. A convict, a thief. She needed someone mature, steady, decent."

"So when you saw him running away after the fight, it seemed logical to you that he was the one who'd killed her."

"Not then, no. I didn't know anyone had killed anyone. I'd run downstairs, shouting to them to stop, but I don't think they heard me. I ran back up here to phone the police, but then it went quiet. I was giving myself a belt of nerve-steadier in the kitchen, when I saw him run across the patio. Hop. He was trying to put on his pants. He was stark naked. I remember laughing."

"He was bleeding," Dave said.

"I didn't see that. Later, the police showed me the blood-smears on the windowsill, and the drops across the patio, but I didn't notice it when he ran off."

"You didn't phone the police?"

"What for?" Stancliff shrugged. "It was over."

"Completely," Dave said. "You didn't go downstairs to check whether she was all right?"

Stancliff looked away. "I should have, shouldn't I? The truth is, I'd been working around the clock to meet a deadline—not eating, keeping myself going on coffee and uppers. And that double Scotch hit me like a two-by-four. I passed out.

When I came to, it was dark. That didn't bother me so much as the silence. I was used to hearing her music all the time. The silence was eerie. It worried me. So then I did go down to see if she was all right."

"And she was dead," Dave said.

"And she was dead." Pain muffled Stancliff's words. Tears wet his eyes. "She was a wonderful, beautiful person. She'd had a rotten run of luck, but that was over. Marvelous talent." He gave a soundless, sorry laugh. "I thought I wanted that once—talent. Not for music, for art. But from what I've seen, it involves too much suffering. Read their lives. Talented people have a miserable time of it."

Dave opened the door. "I'll bring the key back," he said, and went out and closed the door.

The curtains were drawn, so the light was dim. He found pull ropes and rattled the curtains open. The twelve string guitar lay on a coffee table. It was blotched with fingerprint powder. So were the room's other surfaces. The guitar was all that showed anyone special had lived here. That and the big reel-to-reel tape recorder. Its brightwork caught the light. He put on reading glasses, switched on amplifier and tape deck, and set the reels turning. Bargain loudspeakers sat on a dusty hardwood floor. From the speakers came a sweet, steady voice singing lyrics that rhymed "protects" with "MX" as in missile. Rader exaggerated. Nervously was how she managed the twelve-string. Dave switched off the system and tucked away his glasses.

Nothing had been tidied in the kitchen. Tins that had held TV dinners lay in the sink, a faucet dripping into them. There were soiled forks. Empty diet soft-drink cans stood on the counter beside the sink. Cupboard doors hung slightly open. Inside waited a few clean plates, drinking glasses, mugs. The empty shelves were just that—empty. So was the refrigerator freezer compartment, whose ice cube tray held only ice cubes. The main part of the refrigerator contained a carton of skim milk, a six pack of diet cola, a jar of grapefruit juice. The wastebasket under the sink was stuffed with stained hamburger wrappers, pizza tins, fried chicken buckets, more soft drink cans. The stove top wore a film of dust.

The bedroom held bed, chest, mirror, lamp, clock. The bed had been stripped. The police lab would have wanted a look at Rader's bloodstains. The closet contained mostly jeans and blouses, a couple of skirts, no dresses. Bright colors, though—brave, humorous. A pair of shiny fake leather boots, worn Adidases, no carton of clippings. In the chest of drawers, sweaters, gaudy T-shirts, pantyhose, a couple of bras in boxes yet to be opened. Penney's, Woolworth's. Nothing uncommon in the bathroom medicine cabinet—aspirin, cold capsules, antacid tablets, tampons. Only one prescription drug—a folder of contraceptive pills. No forbidden drugs. No syringes, needles, rubber tubing. He closed the mirrored door, and stretched to run his hand along the top of the cabinet. A dusty key, the flat kind, stamped out. Nothing to identify it except a number, twenty three. He dropped it into his pocket.

Under the lid of the toilet tank he found no plastic envelopes of cocaine, heroin, marijuana, PCP, Quaaludes. No drugs lay anchored in balloons in the bottom of the tank. In the clothes hamper, a tall basket woven of split bamboo, was nothing but dirty laundry. He crouched and opened the vanity doors under the wash basin. Toilet bowl cleaner, air freshener, a flat, dry, blue cellulose sponge, a pink-bristled toilet bowl brush, two bars of bath soap. He unwrapped these to be sure. The perfume of the soap was strong. He felt around carefully in the dark corners behind pipes under the basin. Nothing. He closed the doors, rose, switched off the light, left the bathroom.

When he stepped into the livingroom again, he thought he saw for an instant a face at the window. He went to the window. Nothing stirred outside. The landscaping was desert plants set in coarse white gravel. No one hurried off up the sunny street on foot. Not a car moved. He turned back, frowning. If not to buy drugs, why had someone brought Bess Jessup five thousand dollars in small bills? He sat on a smudged couch and lifted the guitar from the coffee table. When he laid it on the floor, its strings hummed.

The table was strewn with music manuscript and blue-lined notebook pages. On these, in ballpoint pen, were written the words of songs. Dave put on his reading glasses again. Her subjects were Three Mile Island, Times Beach, and how war kills children. He laid music and words aside, pushed away glossy campaign mailers, *Catton for Congress*. Beneath lay letters with the logos of recording companies. What the letters indicated was that Bess Jessup had sent reminders of her long-lapsed career, along with new audition tapes, to a number of places that didn't care.

And to one that did. A little bit. Jawal Singh was cautiously friendly. He was president of Seesaw Records. His letter Dave folded and pushed into a pocket. He put away his glasses, closed the curtains, locked the apartment, and returned the door key to Stancliff. The found key he showed the gaunt man who took it in white gloved fingers, frowning. "Belong to anything of yours?" Dave asked.

"Never saw it before," Stancliff said. "You want it?"

"For a little while," Dave said.

He was a few steps down the concrete strip between the white-gravelled plantings when he heard a hiss behind him. He turned. At a corner of the building, a worried-looking man made a beckoning gesture. He wore a Levi outfit he was too fat for, and a billed cap with *Dr Pepper* stitched on its front. Behind the man, a VW van's windshield reflected the sun. It was noon, and the sun was hot by now. Dave crunched across the gravel to the man, who whispered:

"Brandstetter? The insurance man?"

"That's me." Dave handed him a card.

"Harvey Sweetzer," the man said. "They told me at the insurance company office that you'd be coming here. Something wrong? Aren't we going to get the money?" He kept looking past Dave up and down the street, and he hurried his words. "I really need that money. For my business."

"I know," Dave said. A fat woman was staring at him through the windshield of the van. She wore sunglasses, but neither these nor the fleshiness of her cheeks hid her likeness to her dead sister, of whom the police had photographs Dave had seen. "Why did someone toss her apartment?"

"What?" Sweetzer said. "What?"

"The landlord said that when he found your sister-in-law's body, the apartment was a wreck, everything thrown every which way. Why?"

"How the hell would I know?" Sweetzer said. "We didn't associate with her. We're not that kind of people."

"She kept a box of clippings. It's not in the police report, and it's not in the apartment."

"Probably old stuff from when she was a singer. She had a start, you know." The door of the van opened. Sweetzer turned. "Carolyn, never mind." He said to Dave, "Then the Vietnam war ended, and all that radical stuff dried up. And first it was drugs, then prostitution. A hooker." He wagged his head glumly. "My own wife's sister."

"You didn't take the clippings? You didn't tear the apartment up, looking for this key? She had it hidden."

"Me?" Sweetzer's eyes opened as wide as the pouches of fat around them allowed. "We've never even been here. Look—when do we get the check? I've got a lot of people I owe money to, breathing down my neck."

Carolyn called from the van, "We can't even show

our faces, can't open the cafe, can't even go home." She sounded on the verge of tears. "You have to help us."

"The check won't be sent until I clear it," Dave said, "and I have a lot of questions about your sister's death."

"That no-good convict kid stabbed her," Sweetzer said. "The one she was living with, sleeping with. Ex-druggie, like herself. That's how that kind of people live. That's how she'd been living for fifteen years. What are you talking about? What questions?"

"If she was so contemptible," Dave said, "why did you keep up the payments on her life insurance? You didn't want anything to do with her. You never came to see her. She was trying to start a new life, no more drugs, no more prostitution. She'd been through rehabilitation. She was writing songs, trying for a record deal. You didn't care."

Sweetzer's laugh was sour and pitying. "You don't know much about those kind of people, I guess. You know how many times she'd told Carolyn and me she was through with all that sordid stuff, she was going to start over with her music and all that? So many times I lost count."

Now Carolyn did clamber down from the van. A scarf was tied over her head. Her fat hips were packed into jeans. She came at a ding-toed walk to stand beside her husband. "We helped her. Helped her again and again. We never knew in the middle of the night when the phone would ring, and she'd be in jail again, or at some hospital, and crying for us to come and bail her out, or whatever."

"That's why I took out the life insurance,"

Sweetzer said. "Because the way she was living—hell, she was living with a black man, did you know that?—anybody with a grain of sense knew she was going to end up dead one of these times. Murdered. It was in the cards."

"We tried to save her." Tears leaked from under Carolyn's dark glasses. "We brought her from jail that time, to live with us, her own room and all. Gave her a job waitressing at the cafe."

Sweetzer snorted. "How long do you think that lasted?"

Carolyn blew her nose loudly on a Kleenex.

"We're her only family," Sweetzer said. "We'd have to bury her when the day came. That's why I kept up the policy."

"Fifty thousand dollars will buy a lot of funeral," Dave said.

"Listen," Sweetzer said, "I don't add up what I do out of the goodness of my heart. But we're not rich people, and over the years we emptied our pockets for her, paid her back rent, utilities, got her guitar out of hock, paid her bailbondsmen, paid her fines. When it's your own wife's sister, you do what you have to do. You think I'm some kind of mean, grasping guy, wanting this insurance money. Well, I never asked her for a dime back, when she was alive."

"You have to help us," Carolyn said. "We're being hounded like we were animals. We have to sleep in the van. People can only keep that up so long."

Dave said, "Where do you park it to sleep in it?"

Sweetzer shrugged. "Beach. Out of the way places."

"The night she was killed?" Dave said.

"Oh, my goodness." Carolyn took a step backward.

Sweetzer tried to sound truculent but he only squeaked. "What the hell do you mean by that?" Sweat broke out on his upper lip. "Are you accusing us?"

"No, but I don't think Mike Rader killed her," Dave said. "He didn't have a reason."

"And we do?" Carolyn cried. "My own sister?"

"Drugs addicts don't need reasons," Sweetzer said.

"The tests show he's clean of drugs," Dave said.

"We were in Griffith Park. We weren't in anybody's way. Couldn't even be seen from the road. But the patrol found us and rousted us out," Sweetzer said in disgust.

"What time was that?" Dave said.

"Let's go, Carolyn." Sweetzer took her fat arm and steered her ahead of him back to the van. "We don't have to answer his questions."

"It will be on the park patrol records," Dave said. "You may as well tell me. Or won't it be on the records?"

"Yeah." Sweetzer pushed Carolyn up into the van. "It's on the damn records. They issued us a citation. We haven't got enough troubles. A little after seven." He slammed the passenger door, and walked around to the driver's side. He opened the door there. "Who do I go to at that insurance company to get some action?"

"I never heard of anyone like that at an insurance company," Dave said.

Dave entered Max Romano's restaurant through the kitchen as usual. The air was hot and steamy, heady with smells of garlic, parmesan, basil. He gave a lift of the hand to the somber, gaunt head chef Alex, spoke the names of the other kitchen help, and pushed into the restaurant that hummed and clinked with conversation, eating, drinking. Max drew a good lunch-time crowd. Dave glanced toward the corner table Max always reserved for him. He expected to see Cecil Harris waiting there. A television news field reporter, Cecil was young, black, gangly as a basketball player. He lived with Dave. But he wasn't sitting at the corner table. Hats Jimmerson was, a huge hulk of a man in a shiny black mohair suit, green shirt, wide flame—colored necktie. Max Romano appeared at Dave's elbow, clutching menus, worried.

"I'm sorry," he said. "He insisted."

"You did the right thing," Dave said. Heart pounding, he edged his way between tables. Jimmerson glowered at him. Dave said, "What the hell does this mean?"

"It mean," Jimmerson rumbled, "never send a boy on a man's errand. How can anybody so smart act so stupid? Sit down. You attracting attention. I don't need that."

"Where is Cecil?" Dave said.

"I said, sit down. If you do like I say in every way, Cecil going to be okay." Jimmerson looked at a wristwatch studded with diamonds. Diamonds glittered in rings on his thick fingers. "I expect he is enjoying lunch at this moment with some of my people. Barbecued ribs? Barbecued chicken? I forget today's menu."

Dave sat down because his legs felt weak. Cecil's assignment had been only to locate Jimmerson. Dave had warned him not to go near the man, not to take any risks. Jimmerson was right. Dave had been stupid. Max came now and set down a stocky glass of Glenlivet on the rocks. He and Dave had been friends for almost forty years. They always exchanged small talk. Not today. Max hovered for a nervous moment, then went doubtfully away.

"What did he do?" Dave tasted the Scotch. "Come ring your doorbell?"

Jimmerson shook his head. "He was just asking too many people too many questions. I have a great many friends. One of them was bound to phone me up. Just because a man is black don't mean he'll go unnoticed in the black community. I assume you were thinking along those lines?"

"Something like that," Dave said. "And he's a good investigator. He told you why I wanted to locate you?"

Jimmerson's drink was green. He took a sip of it and nodded. "Yes. You want to clear a young prevaricator of a murder charge against a lady I once knew."

"Were you there?" Dave said. "For my information only. I won't make any trouble for you. I don't want Cecil hurt."

Jimmerson said slowly and distinctly, "I have not laid eyes on Bess Jessup since we split up two years ago, when they busted her for dealing cocaine. I didn't even know she was out of prison, let alone where she was living. And don't jive me, Mr. Brandstetter, please. Wherever you go, trouble ain't but two, three steps behind."

"You know where everybody's living," Dave said.

"Including you." Jimmerson picked up a hat from the carpet. It was shiny black straw with a wide brim and a cerise plume wrapped around the band. "It so happen"—he got to his feet; he was a good six foot five, a good three hundred pounds—"that on that afternoon, with twenty other distinguished guests, I was having cocktails with the President at the Annenberg estate in Palm Springs."

"The district attorney wants Mike Rader dead," Dave said. "He's no boy scout, but he doesn't deserve that."

"He be all right." Jimmerson put on the hat and smiled. A diamond glittered in each of his incisors. "He got a friend. That what we all of us need in this life. Friends. That why the po-lice have such a lot of bad luck when it come to me. See, the police, they just naturally ain't got no friends." He chuckled, picked up his glass, finished off the green drink, set the glass down, licked his lips. "But me— I got nothing but friends. That way the po-lice didn't look very hard for me when this felonious child told them his story. That why you shouldn't have put your skinny young associate to the trouble. The day Bess Jessup lost her life, I was with my friends. It don't matter which of my friends gets asked was I with them—I was with them. All right?"

"Someone brought her five thousand dollars in small bills that day," Dave said. "Any idea who that would be?"

"Not me." The diamonds in Jimmerson's teeth flashed again. "I don't deliver. I collect."

"She owned a box of clippings," Dave said. "It's gone."

"She always had that. It didn't mean nothing. Just old, no-good memories. Trash. Nobody would steal that."

"This mean anything to you?" Dave laid the key down.

Jimmerson frowned at it, turned it over with sparkling fingers. "It a key. Where to? Don't look like much."

Dave put the key away. "When do I see Cecil?"

"Relax. Enjoy your lunch. And I think I can promise you"—Jimmerson consulted the jewelled watch again—"that he will be joining you for dessert."

"Captain Barker will like hearing that," Dave said.

"Give the Captain my regards," Jimmerson said, "and tell him that I am going to be traveling abroad, indefinitely. I think it is time for me to go check on my Swiss bank accounts." He tilted his hat and strolled out. A good many people stopped eating to watch him.

Dave got up to follow and sat down again. But he did not relax, did not enjoy his lunch. He nibbled at the spinach salad, choked down a bite or two of bread, left untouched the best Alfredo in town. He was on his third Scotch, staring into it, disgusted with himself, when Cecil dropped into his customary chair and grinned at him.

"Thank God," Dave said. "They didn't hurt you."

"I don't like barbecue that spicy," Cecil said, "but you better believe I ate it without complaining." He sobered. "Look, I'm sorry I messed up. I thought I was being discreet. Then, all of a sudden, I'm riding off between two gorillas in a long, black limousine, just like on TV. 'Mr. Jimmerson would like a few words with you.' Whoo-ee!"

"Don't apologize," Dave said. "It was my mistake. I'm thankful you came out unscathed. He was there, all right."

"He admitted it?" Cecil looked surprised.

"No, but those cuts on Bess Jessup's face came from his rings—I'd bet on it. If we could search his place, we'd find clothes of his with her blood on them. And Rader's."

"You search his place," Cecil said. "I'll stay home."

"There's no point," Dave said, and watched Max set down a green Heineken bottle and a tall, frosty glass for Cecil. Dave said, "Max? You all right?"

"That man looked like some kind of criminal," Max said. "I was ready to call the police."

"You're a shrewd judge of character," Dave said.

"In this business, you get to know." With a sage nod into his double chins, Max waddled away.

Cecil measured beer into his glass, tasted it, wiped foam from his upper lip. "No point?" he said.

"Hats didn't kill her. Her bruises had time to develop, darken, swell. She was killed later. The body temperature test allows a two-hour leeway. The examiner wrote down five-thirty because Stancliff said that was the time of the fight."

"Hats could have come back," Cecil said. "So could Rader."

"And left without the five thousand dollars?" Dave said.

"You're a shrewd judge of character," Cecil said.

Seesaw Records' offices and studios were on the second floor of a weary brick building in a district where no one swept the sidewalks. Big cardboard cartons of records narrowed a dim hallway at the top of the stairs up from the street. Microphone booms, coiled black rubber cables, leaning guitar cases. Dave stepped around the tarnished carcass of an old Scully tape deck to knock on a door whose cracked opaque glass was lettered with Jawal Singh's name. A high, musical voice told him to come in. The office needed fresh paint. The ceiling showed that, not the walls—they were covered with posters, album jackets, yellowing photographs of singers and instrumentalists, and eight or ten gold records mounted behind dusty plexiglass. A tiny brown man with long, smoky black hair sat at a desk stacked with reels of tape, albums, cassettes, strewn with papers, and little white cartons that had once held Chinese take-out food. The tiny man had big, glistening brown eyes, and dazzling teeth.

"How can I help you?" He rose, held out a tiny hand. TAXIDERMY was lettered across his T-shirt. The elaborate calligraphy had faded. Dave shook the hand. Jawal Singh said, "You don't look like someone in the music business." Dave gave him a card. He read the card, frowned, smiled once more. "I have heard of you. Yes, I think I have even seen you on the television. What an honor. Please sit down."

"Thank you." Dave looked for a chair that wasn't stacked with records, tapes, copies of *Rolling Stone,* and didn't see one. He set the stack from the chair nearest the desk on the floor and sat down. "I've come about Bess Jessup. For the company that insured her life."

"Ah. What a tragedy. A talented girl. I think she was just beginning to get it together." Singh's speech was elegant and precise, a touch of London in it, a memory of Delhi. "She had been through many difficult years. Now she wanted to resume the career that drugs destroyed."

"Also changing times," Dave said

"The world is always surprising us," Singh said. "Who could have guessed that all our marches of protest, our speeches and songs and petitions could have brought about the ending of that war? And by Mr. Nixon! I was totally taken by surprise." He glanced around the woebegone office. "I sometimes wonder if I will ever recover. I was deeply committed to peace. But I was not prepared for it. This operation of mine was not like other record companies. It was a crusade on my part. I chose my artists for the message they had to bring the world. Peace, brotherhood."

"And the world lost interest," Dave said. He nodded at Singh's T-shirt. "Taxidermy?"

"Ah." Singh touched the letters with a sheepish smile. "Yes. They were my one successful bid to break with the crusading past, to enter the world of—what did they call it?—'the me generation'?"

"That's what they called it."

"Taxidermy were very gifted young people. Rock artists. For a little while, they enjoyed great fame and fortune. Regularly they topped the charts." He waved at the gold records. "Those were theirs. It was a time of unwonted prosperity for me." He smiled wistfully for a moment, remembering, then grew mournful. "But they were too young to cope with the success, the money, the adulation. One by one, they destroyed themselves with drugs."

"Are you satisfied that Bess Jessup had really gone off drugs for good? On the night she was killed, someone brought her five thousand dollars. She couldn't have been dealing again?"

"One cannot, of course, predict human behavior," Singh said. "I should be deeply disturbed to think it. But she was having a difficult time raising the required ten thousand dollars for me to produce her new album."

"Is that the custom?" Dave said. "For the artist to put up part of the money?"

"It is the custom when a company is as near extinction as this one." Singh smiled faintly. "And when one knows that human behavior cannot be predicted, particularly that of addictive personalities, however good their intentions."

"In other words," Dave said, "you thought that if she had to raise a bundle to put into the album, it might keep her straight."

Singh nodded. "But not principally. The truth is, I have the recording facilities here, and I have still a fair distribution system, but almost no capital, and certainly no capital to waste." He frowned. "I do hope that she did not resort to drug dealing to raise that money. Guilt for that would be upon me for the rest of my days, doubly so, since it apparently resulted in her death."

"You were going to handle the advertising and publicity too, I suppose," Dave said. "Did she happen to bring you a box of clippings about her career in the sixties?"

"How did you know?" Singh's brows rose.

"It should have been in her apartment and it wasn't."

Singh popped out of his chair. "It is right here." He shifted tapes, albums, and papers off another chair and laid in Dave's hands a department-store suit box. Dave sat down and took off its sunken lid. He found loose clippings, photographs, scrapbooks. The box was too roomy for them. "Please feel free to examine it all. It will show you why she might indeed have come back. She was hoping, once the album was released, to fly to West Germany and join in the protests against the U.S. deployment of missiles there. There it is as it used to be here. Excuse me." He went to the office door. "I have some editing to do. I will be in studio A, if you need me."

"Thank you," Dave said.

When Singh came back, Dave was fitting the lid onto the box. He lifted it once more and took out to show to Singh a newspaper feature, grown yellow around its edges, cracked at its folds. There was a photograph three columns wide. It showed a platform filled with war protest celebrities. Peace posters waved in the picture's foreground. Banners hung over the platform and along its edge. Bess Jessup stood at a microphone with her guitar, her hair blowing in the wind. A young man, tall, slender, fair, stood beside her, clutching a sheaf of papers. Dave pointed him out to Singh. "You think that's the same Jack Catton who's now running for Congress?"

Singh nodded. "I asked her that very question. She said yes, but so bitterly that I regretted having spoken. She and Jack Catton were lovers, then. They lived together. Both were very active in the anti-war movement. He earned his living as a journalist for the *Free Press, Open City*, the other counter-culture papers—all vanished now." Singh's laugh was sad. "How long ago that was."

"Maybe not," Dave said.

Catton came at a long-legged stride up the brightly lighted airport tunnel from the Sacramento four o'clock shuttle flight. He was in a crowd of other passengers, but he stood out. For one thing, he was taller. For another, his hair shone brassy as a new trumpet. He was handsome, and his pace, the way he swung his attaché case, spelled energy. Here was a man not just leaving an aircraft and heading for office or home. Here was a man going someplace important. He'd put on weight since the sixties, but he was still trim. A plump young woman hurried along beside him on short legs. He talked to her. Rapidly. Dave stepped into his way, handed him a card.

"Mr. Catton? Dave Brandstetter. Can I talk to you?"

Catton blinked at him, at the card. "Insurance? I'm sorry. I have all I need." He started to step around Dave.

"I'm a death claims investigator," Dave said. "It's about Elizabeth Jessup. Bess. You used to know her."

Catton's skin had a childlike transparency. He blushed. He looked sharply at the plump girl. "Lucy—go phone and say the flight was late. I'm running behind. I'll be there as soon as I can. Wait for me at the car, okay?"

"I'll bring it around," she said. "Don't be long, Jack. It's the mayor, remember." She looked harried, sweaty, rumpled, but she summoned a smile for Dave. "Try not to keep him long," she pleaded.

"Let's go to the coffee shop," Catton said.

"The bar will be less crowded," Dave said.

Catton drank Perrier water. "All I know about it is that she was murdered. Her lover stabbed her. I really don't have time to read a newspaper these days. When I see television it's because it's going in a room I'm running through. I'm sorry she's dead. She meant a lot to me once. Everything. But that was in megalithic times."

Dave drank Scotch—not very good Scotch but it was all there was. "Why did the two of you break up?"

Catton read his watch. "Dear God, that was nineteen seventy, man. Fourteen years ago. I haven't seen her since. I was in New York for five years—"

"In journalism," Dave said. "Starting with the *Village Voice*, and branching out to the national liberal weeklies—the *Nation*, the *New Republic*. It got you name recognition." Dave had spent an hour researching Catton at the library after leaving Jawal Singh. "Then, when you decided to go into politics, you came back to Los Angeles."

"It was home," Catton said. "My roots are here."

"First the Gene McCarthy presidential campaign, then the school board, then the state assembly, now congress. And you never looked up Bess Jessup? Why not?"

"I heard what had happened to her." Catton looked somber. "Drugs, prostitution, prison." He gazed at the far glass wall, beyond which glossy white jet liners taxied white runways. "Anyway, we were through. She was a dreamer. I was"—his smile was thin, one-cornered—"into action, right? And we'd both been very young. I thought we believed in the same ideals. But for her, it was all just a big emotional high."

"You were into all of it," Dave said, "from draft-card burning to women's lib, even the black activists." Dave smiled slightly, eyeing Catton's blondness. "Ideals? Not just politics—building for your future?"

"This isn't getting us anyplace. What do you want?"

Dave told Catton Bess Jessup's story. "She wasn't having much luck raising the money. Some of your campaign literature was on her coffee table. I wondered if she'd come to you for a loan."

Catton stared. "Are you serious? She hated me. Two people never broke up with less chance of ever getting together again. Come to me for money? Bess? No way."

"You didn't feel sorry for her and take her five thousand dollars out of your campaign fund? Cash? Small bills? In a supermarket sack? You didn't deliver it?"

"I'm not listening to any more." Catton snatched up his briefcase from an empty chair and stood. "You go tell whoever sent you that trying to link my name to Bess Jessup's now isn't going to do a damn bit of good. I haven't seen her. If she did come to me, I'd refuse to see her. I'm sorry she's had a rough life, but it's also been a well-publicized life, and every story was more squalid than the last. And I'm not having my name connected to a woman like that. No politician would." He started off again.

"No one sent me." Dave fell in beside him. "I'm investigating her murder, that's all. If there's no need to bring your name into it, I won't bring it in."

"Believe me," Catton snarled, "there's no need."

"Whoever brought her that money," Dave said, "also ransacked her apartment. Can you suggest why?"

"Obviously looking for drugs," Catton said. He pushed out through glass doors to a broad sidewalk busy with luggage carts, with men, women, children arriving, departing. Cars inched along, bumper to bumper, or paused at curbside, unloading passengers and baggage. "There's my ride," Catton said.

"One last thing." Dave held out the key. "I found this hidden in her apartment. She kept souvenirs from the past. Is this one? Does it recall anything to you?"

Catton snatched it, scowling, turned it over in his hand, gave it back. "Nothing. Now, will you excuse me, please? I have a very important appointment." He ran toward a shiny black Seville at the curb. The plump young woman, who leaned across to open the passenger door for him, looked ready to weep with impatience.

Dave dropped the key back into his pocket.

One look at the airport terminal lockers showed him the key wouldn't work in their doors. He took the long way home from the airport and stopped at the Greyhound bus station in Santa Monica. The key went grudgingly into the lock of number twenty three, but it wouldn't turn. It almost refused to come loose again. Dusk had reached the canyon before him. High overhead the sky held transparent blue-green light, but down here between the shaggy, shadowy hills, cars had to climb the crooked road with their headlights on. It was night for sure by the time Dave jounced down into his yard off Horseshoe Canyon Road. His headlights flared back at him from the long row of French doors that fronted his odd house. He parked the Jaguar, switched off the lights, climbed wearily out. He rounded the front building, and crossed the un-even bricks of the courtyard under a dark, spread-ing oak whose dry leaves crackled beneath his shoes. He switched on lights in the cookshack and built himself a double martini. He would carry it across to the back building where, this morning, he had readied kindling and logs in the big fireplace. With the setting of the sun, October had asserted itself. A chill was in the air. He turned off the cookshack lights, stepped out, carrying the icy drink, and pulled the door shut behind him. He took two steps in the familiar dark. At his back, someone else took a step. He made a sharp half turn. Something hard struck his skull. He went down. The splintering of glass was the last thing he heard for a long time.

"All that blood." Cecil stood at the foot of the bed where Dave sat propped on pillows feeling wan in the morning sunshine that poured down from a skylight not far above him in the raftered, plank roof of the sleeping loft. "When I got here at midnight, and saw all that blood, I thought you were dead for sure." He set a bentwood breakfast tray on Dave's knees. "But where were you? I phoned everybody, before I had the sense to look up here. And here you were, sleeping like a little child, head all wrapped in white."

"Nothing bleeds like a scalp wound," Dave said. "I didn't notice the mess I was making. I had to telephone. The paramedics got here in no time. After I was stitched up, the hospital wanted to keep me overnight, but I took a taxi back here. I didn't phone you at work because I didn't want to upset you. Instead, the blood did that."

"Drink the orange juice," Cecil said. "Drink the coffee. You need liquids to replace the blood."

Dave frowned around him. "What went with my clothes?"

"I stuffed them in a plastic bag. They're ruined.".

"Look in the left pocket of the jacket," Dave said.

Cecil went down the raw pine plank steps from the loft. He was gone for a few minutes. Dave drank the orange juice. His stomach almost turned over, but not quite. He tried the coffee. Cautiously. That was better. Cecil climbed back up the stairs. "Nothing in the left pocket. Nothing in any of the pockets. Stole your watch, your wallet, your checkbook—even your reading glasses. Why would they leave anything in your pockets?"

"They only wanted the key," Dave said.

The light had changed when Dave woke again. He was sweating. The noon sun beating down on the roof made the loft hot. The smell of pine lumber was strong, and underlying it was a faint memory of hay and horse: these buildings he called home had once been stables. He had tried earlier to get out of bed. His head had reacted badly. He tried again now, tentatively, a few inches at a time. If he took it slow, it felt as if it would be all right. He got to the stairs. They appeared to swim. He gripped the rail until the dizziness stopped. Then he made his way carefully down to the bathroom. When he came out of the bathroom, Cecil had returned and was standing, studying him, worried.

"You look sick." He took Dave's arm. "Back to bed."

"What did you find?" Dave said.

"You were right. She chose the place nearest to where she lived—the Trailways depot. But they'd been and gone. Key was in the lock. Inside looked empty." Cecil's support was welcome. Dave seemed to want to fall over. "And I started to leave it, when I saw a piece of paper. It was stuck in the weld at the back. Half a piece of paper."

"Let me see it," Dave said.

"When we've got you up these stairs," Cecil said.

It was an old photocopy, discolored and sooty. Part of a letter. Happily, the part that bore the letterhead. STUDENTS AGAINST WAR. And the date, 15 August 1970. Dave missed his reading glasses, but by squinting he made out some of the typing. The sense of it was lost in the past, however. It was a fragment from the middle of some ongoing plan of action—a rally, a demonstration, a march? Dave studied the letterhead again. The address was on Vermont Avenue, near City College. But Students Against War wouldn't be there now. Students Against War wouldn't be anywhere now. A list of officers ran partway down the left edge of the page in tiny type. Dave handed the paper to Cecil.

"Can you read those names?"

Cecil read them to him. Dave smiled.

Andy Levitan had freckles and kinky red hair. Dave knew him because he was a junior partner of Abe Greenglass, Dave's attorney. He didn't know him well, merely to speak to. But Dave had asked Abe Greenglass to send Andy Levitan to his house. Now he sat on the edge of Dave's bed and frowned through hornrim glasses with very large, round lenses, at the torn scrap of letterhead, and smiled with irony, and slowly shook his head. He handed the paper back.

"Where the hell did you get that?"

"Bess Jessup had it," Dave said.

"I saw where she was murdered. You looking into that?"

"Was she part of Students Against War?" Dave said.

"She sang at all our rallies, but she wasn't a member. Boy, I never expected to see that letterhead again. That was a thousand years ago. 'Andy Levitan, Executive Secretary.' How seriously we took ourselves." He tilted his head at Dave, forehead creased. "You think this had something to do with her death? How could that be? Anyway, what was she doing with it?"

"I was hoping you could tell me," Dave said.

"I thought we destroyed every piece of paper in

that office," Levitan said. "In one very large, very hasty bonfire. You see, we'd planned a major assault on the system—a raid on a draftboard, to burn their records."

Cecil whistled. "What happened?"

"It was a close secret, all right? But somebody told the police, and they were there, waiting for us in the dark. Surprise! They let us splash the kerosene around, almost let us light the match, before they switched on the lights. We got out on bail, but we figured we were done for, that we'd spend the rest of our lives in prison. They'd sealed our offices, put a guard on, but we broke in the back and stole our own files and destroyed them."

"You had a spy in your midst," Dave said.

Levitan nodded. "Bob Broughton. It had to be him. He didn't get prosecuted—'insufficient evidence.' After which he joined the Marines. Jack Catton wanted to kill him." Levitan's laugh was short and bleak. "As it turned out, Vietnam killed him."

Behind a sprawling tudor style house, very black beams, mullioned windows, very white plaster, a long lawn sloped down to a lake with swans and rushes. Trees threw lacy shade on the grass, and on colorful flowerbeds. The women were colorful too, in picture hats against the blazing sun. The men wore summer whites. Left-liberal campaign contributors, they held drinks and little bowls of strawberries in clotted cream. Untidy rows of folding chairs had been abandoned—the politicking was over. Dave spotted Catton and moved through the chatting, laughing crowd to stand waiting for him to quit scattering charm for a moment. When he did, Dave stepped in.

"What happened to you?" Catton frowned. "Accident?"

"Impatience," Dave said. "Not mine. Someone else's. They wanted that key I showed you, and they must have assumed I wouldn't give it to them if they simply asked."

"What did they want with it?" Catton led Dave aside. "I had the idea you didn't know what it was for."

"I do now. It fit a locker in a bus station. Not far from where Bess Jessup lived."

"That was where she had the drugs hidden?"

"Not drugs." Dave's head pounded. The heat was punishing. "A bunch of photocopies of documents from the nineteen-sixties—when you two lived together."

Catton looked blank. "Documents?"

"Letters from outfits like Students Against War."

Catton expelled a short, bewildered laugh. "Why would Bess have hung onto junk like that?"

"You tell me. You were in Students Against War."

"So were hundreds of decent kids." Catton looked worriedly across the lawn, as if afraid of missing a chance to shake a hand. "What could it have to do with her death?"

"The five thousand wasn't for drugs," Dave said. "So what does that leave?"

"What? Sorry. Excuse me." Catton started away, up the grassy slope. "There's councilman Greevey."

"Wait," Dave said. "It leaves blackmail, right?"

"You've lost me," Catton said. Then his expression changed. "Hell, we destroyed the SAW papers. You see—"

"Andy Levitan told me," Dave said. "But obviously some escaped. He figures the police spy made copies, and somehow Bess got hold of them. But he says the spy was Bob Broughton, and Broughton is dead. You can't blackmail a dead man."

"So it wasn't blackmail." Catton started off again.

"Unless the spy was someone else," Dave said. "Maybe all of you were mistaken about Broughton. It would be nice to know, wouldn't it?"

Catton halted, turned back. "There's no way. The police department is being sued right now. For undercover activities against political organizations." His smile was wry. "They never stop, do they? But it means the records will be sealed."

"Not to everyone," Dave said. "I'll have Captain Ken Barker check them for me. He's an old friend. And he owes me. He's out of town today, but he'll be back tomorrow. I'll phone you, shall I? When he gives me the name?"

Catton was staring at Dave, but without seeing him. "What? Oh, yes. I mean, no." He made a despairing gesture with his hand. "Don't bother. I'll be honest with you. I took her the five thousand. Yes, she came to me and begged. You were right— I felt sorry for her. I felt even sorrier for her when I saw her at that miserable, torn-up apartment. Her face was a mass of cuts and bruises. But there was no blackmail. You can forget that part. And she was alive when I left her, soaking her face with cold towels."

"What time?" Dave said.

"A little after seven." Catton laid a trembling hand on Dave's arm. "You won't let it come out, will you? What I said at the airport was true—a candidate connected with a woman like that: voters wouldn't understand. At the scene of a murder, the night it happened? It would finish me. And what good would it do Bess?"

"I'll telephone you with that name," Dave said.

It was colder tonight, and damp. Rain was due. At sundown, clouds had blown in from the sea. They hung low and thick over the canyon now and made the darkness beneath the old oak complete. A bench circled the stout trunk of the oak. Ordinarily plants in pots occupied the bench, but Dave had set some of them on the ground. He sat on the bench, back against the oak, and waited. He wore two sweaters and a coat with a sheepskin lining, but the cold got through. He shivered, his head hurt, and he kept falling asleep.

He jerked awake and pushed up the thick sleeve at his wrist to read his new watch. Ten past ten. Had he been wrong? It wouldn't be the first time, but it would surprise hell out of him. He pushed his cold hands into the slash pockets of the coat and dozed off again. He couldn't make out what woke him the next time. He looked at the front building, where he had left lamps on and a classical music station playing through the stereo. He wished he was in there with the fire blazing and a big globe of brandy.

He read his watch again. Five of eleven. The hell

with it. He got up stiffly from the bench, yawned, started to raise his arms to stretch, when head-lights beams crossed the dark, shaggy heads of the trees out front. The underside of a car scraped paving. Dave smiled thinly. He was always mean-ing to get the humpy drop from the road into his yard graded. The glow of the headlights beyond the front building winked out. A car door closed. Dave stepped behind the trunk of the oak.

There was no scuffing of shoes on the bricks. The soles must be soft. But they still crackled dry leaves. Dave listened to them. A man appeared in silhou-ette against the door to the front building, a heavy old door with thick squares of glass. Something was odd-looking about the man's head. It took a sec-ond to understand—he was wearing a ski mask. He lifted a hand to press the button in the frame of the door. But he didn't use a finger or a thumb. He used the barrel of a gun. It glinted in the light that came out through the door. Dave launched himself at the man, caught his arm. He meant to twist the arm behind the man's back, make him drop the gun.

The man was stronger than he was. He used the leverage of Dave's grip on his arm to slam Dave hard against the shingle wall of the building. Dave's head met the wall with a crack. The pain was blinding. He went down. "You have to under-stand," the man said. Dave couldn't understand anything. He was only very dimly aware of being hauled to his feet, of the door opening, of himself a stagger of unaccountable legs into the room where the softly glowing lamps reeled around him, slowly, sickeningly. He sprawled on a couch. "You have to understand," the man said again, and pulled off the ski mask.

"Ah," Dave said hollowly, trying to push himself into a sitting posture. "It is you."

"You're going to die," Catton said, "but you have to understand how it was. He sat on a couch that faced the one where Dave was. A coffee table was between them, Mexican pottery on it, painted terracotta, a wide-eyed cat with its paws tucked up, three jars of different sizes. "They had me on a dope charge. Marijuana. I was selling it on campus at LACC. They were going to lock me up forever. Unless I told them what was going on inside the movement."

"I'm in too much pain to cry," Dave said. "Let me tell you. Bess found out you were spying on your friends, selling out the peaceniks. That's why you left so suddenly for New York. She told you if you didn't go, she'd expose you. She loved you, or she'd have done it regardless."

"She hated me," Catton said. "I never saw such hate."

"Did you know she had a stack of material you'd stolen from Students Against War and the rest?"

"Not until she came to me last week. Asking for ten thousand dollars to pay that racketeering record producer. When I gave it to her, she'd give me the papers." Catton's laugh was bitter. "Everybody sells out. It just takes some of us a little longer."

"You only took her five thousand," Dave said.

Catton shrugged sourly. "What the hell. She was

on her beam ends, a drug addict, a whore. Five thousand would look like a fortune to her."

"Why did you kill her?" Dave said.

"It was an accident. It was her fault. That rotten temper of hers. I asked her for the documents, and she wouldn't give them up. She said she had them hidden in a safe place, and until I brought her the rest of the money, they'd stay there. I started tearing the place apart to find them, and she picked up this switchblade and went for me."

"And you tried to take it away from her?"

"We struggled. Some pimp had beat hell out of her but she was strong. The blade slid into her. I don't know how." Catton stared away numbly. "Christ, I didn't mean to kill her."

"But you went wearing gloves," Dave said. "Your prints aren't on that money. They're not on the sack."

"Just so she couldn't prove I gave it to her and wreck my campaign. I tell you, I never meant to hurt her."

"Only to save yourself," Dave said. "I understand."

"So do I," Ken Barker said. He came from behind the shadowy bar at the upper end of the long room. "Perfectly."

Catton scrambled to his feet and fired his gun. But wildly. Barker's gun went off at almost the same moment, and the impact of the bullet spun Catton around. He fell across the coffee table, knocking the Mexican pottery off, shattering it. He slumped from table to floor and lay still. Dave saw blood. Barker, a big-shouldered man with a broken nose and steel-gray hair, knelt over Catton, laid fingers on the candidate's neck below the jaw hinge. He looked up at Dave. "He's alive. Can you use a phone?"

"I can try." Dave pushed dizzily to his feet, tottered a few steps, picked up a receiver, punched buttons. While the phone rang at the other end of the line, Cecil came through the door at a run. That would make it midnight, the hour he always arrived home from work. Raindrops sparkled in his hair, and his eyes were round with alarm.

"Fourth of July in here?" he said.

"Election day," Dave said.

The Anderson Boy

Prothero, fastening the pegs of his car coat, pushed out through the heavy doors of the Liberal Arts building, and saw the Anderson boy. The boy loped along in an Army surplus jacket and Army surplus combat boots, a satchel of books on his back. His hair, as white and shaggy as when he was five, blew in the cold wind.

He was a long way off. Crowds of students hurried along the paths under the naked trees between lawns brown and patched with last week's snow. But Prothero picked out the Anderson boy at once and with sickening certainty.

Prothero almost ran for his car. When he reached it, in the gray cement vastness of Parking Building B, his hands shook so that he couldn't at first fit the key into the door. Seated inside, he shuddered. His sheepskin collar was icy with sweat crystals. He shut his eyes, gripped the wheel, leaned his head against it.

This was not possible. The trip to promote his book—those staring airport waiting rooms, this plane at midnight, that at four A.M.; snatches of sleep in this and that hotel room; this bookseller luncheon, that radio call-in program; dawns for the Today Show and Good Morning, America, yawns for Johnny Carson; Los Angeles in ninety degree heat, Denver in snow, Chicago in wind, New York in rain; pills to make him sleep, pills to wake him up; martinis, wine, Scotch, poured down him like water—three weeks of it had been too much. His nerves were frayed. He was seeing things. The very worst things.

He drove off campus. By the shopping center, he halted for a red light. He thought about his lecture. It had gone well, which was surprising, tired as he was. But he'd been happy to be back where he belonged, earning an honest living, doing what he loved. Promotion tours? Never again. His publisher was pleased. The book was selling well. But Donald Prothero was a wreck.

The Anderson boy loped across in front of him. He shut his eyes, drew a deep breath, opened his eyes and looked again. He was still sure. Yet how could it be? It was thirteen years since he'd last seen him, and more than a thousand miles from here. On that night, the boy had been a pale little figure in pajamas, standing wide-eyed in the dark breezeway outside the sliding glass wall of his bedroom, hugging a stuffed toy kangaroo. Prothero, in his panicked flight, naked, clutching his clothes, had almost run him over.

The boy had to have recognized him. Prothero was always around. He'd taught the boy to catch a ball, to name birds, lizards, cacti, to swim in the bright blue pool just beyond that breezeway. Prothero had given him the toy kangaroo. He should have stopped. Instead, he'd kept running. He was only eighteen. Nothing bad had ever happened to him. Sick and sweating, he'd driven far into the desert. On some lost, moonlit road, half overgrown by chaparral, he'd jerked into his clothes, hating his body.

He'd known what he had to do—go to the sheriff. He'd started the car again, but he couldn't make himself do it. He couldn't accept what had happened. Things like that took place in cheap books and bad movies, or they happened to sleazy people on the TV news. Not to people like the Andersons. Not to people like him. It could wreck his whole life. He went home. To his room. As always. But he couldn't sleep. All he could do was vomit. His father, bathrobe, hair rumpled, peered at him in the dusky hall when Prothero came out of the bathroom for the third time.

"Have you been drinking?"

"You know better than that."

"Shall we call the doctor?"

"No, I'm all right now."

But he would never be all right again. Next morning, when he stripped to shower, he nearly fainted. His skin was caked with dried blood. He nearly scalded himself, washing it off. He trembled and felt weak, dressing, but he dressed, neat and fresh as always. He kissed his mother and sat on his stool at the breakfast bar, smiling as always. He was a boy who smiled. He'd been senior class president in high school, captain of the basketball team, editor of the yearbook. These things had been handed him, and he'd accepted them without question. As he'd accepted scholarships to University for the coming fall. As he'd accepted his role as Jean Anderson's lover.

His mother set orange juice in front of him, and

his mug with his initial on it, filled with creamy coffee. He knew what she would do next. He wanted to shout at her not to do it. He didn't shout. They would think he was crazy. She snapped on the little red-shelled TV set that hung where she could watch it as she cooked at the burner-deck, where his father and he could watch it while they ate. He wanted to get off the stool and go hide. But they would ask questions. He stayed.

And there on the screen, in black and white, was the Anderson house with its rock roof and handsome plantings, its glass slide doors, the pool with outdoor furniture beside it, the white rail fence. There in some ugly office sat the Anderson boy in his pajamas on a moulded plastic chair under a bulletin-board tacked with papers. The toy kangaroo lay on a floor of vinyl tile among cigarette butts. A pimply-faced deputy bent over the boy, trying to get him to drink from a striped waxpaper cup. The boy didn't cry. He didn't even blink. He sat still and stared at nothing. There were dim, tilted pictures, for a few seconds, of a bedroom, dark blotches on crumpled sheets, dark blotches on pale carpeting Bodies strapped down under blankets were wheeled on gurneys to an ambulance whose rear doors gaped. The Sheriff's face filled the screen, thick, wrinkled eyelids, nose with big pores, cracked lips. He spoke. Then a cartoon tiger ate cereal from a spoon.

"People shouldn't isolate themselves miles from town." Prothero's father buttered toast. "Husband away traveling half the time. Wife and child alone. Asking for trouble."

"He came home." Prothero's mother set plates

of scrambled eggs and bacon on the counter. "It didn't help."

"All sorts of maniacs running loose these days," Prothero's father said. "Evidently no motive. They'll probably never find out who did it."

His father went to his office. His mother went to a meeting of the Episcopal Church altar guild. He drove to the Sheriff's station. He parked on a side street, but he couldn't get out of the car. He sat and stared at the flat-roofed, sand-colored building with the flag pole in front. He ran the radio. At noon, it said the Sheriff had ruled out the possibility of an intruder. The gun had belonged to Anderson. His were the only fingerprints on it. Plainly, there had been a quarrel and Anderson had shot first his wife and then himself. The Anderson boy appeared to be in a state of shock and had said nothing. A grandmother had flown in from San Diego to look after him. Prothero went home to the empty house and cried.

Now, at the intersection, he watched from his car as the boy pushed through glass doors into MacDonald's. He had to be mistaken. This wasn't rational. Horns blared behind him. The light had turned green. He pressed the throttle. The engine coughed and died. Damn. He twisted the key, the engine started, the car bucked ahead half its length and quit again. The light turned orange. On the third try, he made it across the intersection, but the cars he'd kept from crossing honked angrily after him.

The Anderson boy? What made him think that? He'd known a runty little kid. This boy was over six feet tall. A tow-head, yes, but how uncommon was that? He swung the car into the street that would take him home beneath an over-arch of bare tree limbs. The boy looked like his father—but that skull shape, those big, long bones, were simply North European characteristics. Millions of people shared those. The odds were out of the question. It was his nerves. It couldn't be the Anderson boy.

He went from the garage straight to the den, shed the car coat, and poured himself a drink. He gulped down half of it and shivered. The den was cold and smelled shut up. He hadn't come into it yesterday when he got home from the airport. The curtains were drawn. He touched a switch that opened them. Outside, dead leaves stuck to flagging. Winter-brown lawn with neat plantings of birches sloped to a little stream. Woods were gray beyond the stream.

"Ah," Barbara said, "it is you."

"Who else would it be?" He didn't turn to her.

"How did the lecture go?"

"Who built the footbridge?" he said.

"The nicest boy," she said. "A friend of yours from California. Wayne Anderson. Do you remember him?"

"I was going to build it," he said.

"I thought it would be a pleasant surprise for you when you got home. I was saving it." She stepped around stacks of books on the floor and touched him. "You all right?"

"It would have been good therapy for me. Outdoors. Physical labor. Sense of accomplishment."

"He said you'd been so nice to him when he was a little boy. When he saw the lumber piled up down there, and I told him what you had in mind, he said he'd like to do it. And he meant it. He was very quick and handy. Came faithfully every day for a whole week. He's an absolute darling."

Prothero finished his drink. "How much did you have to pay him?"

"He wouldn't let me pay him," she said. "So I fed him. That seemed acceptable. He eats with gusto."

Flakes of snow began to fall. Prothero said, "It's hard to believe."

"He saw you on television in San Diego, but it was tape, and when he phoned the station, you'd gone, of course. He thought you'd come back here. He got on a plane that night." She laughed. "Isn't it wonderful how these children just leap a thousand miles on impulse? Could we even have imagined it at his age? He got our address from Administration and came here without even stopping to unpack. Not that he'd brought much luggage. A duffle-bag is all."

"You didn't invite him to stay," Prothero said.

"I thought of it," she said.

He worked the switch to close the curtains. He didn't want to see the bridge. It was dim in the den and she switched on the desk lamp. He was pouring more whiskey into his glass. He said, "I didn't ask you about Cora last night. How's she doing?"

"It's a miracle. You'd never know she'd had a stroke." He knew from her voice that she was watching him and worried. His hands shook. He spilled whiskey. "You're not all right," she said. "I've never seen you so pale. Don, don't let them talk you into any more book peddling. Please?"

"Is he coming here again?"

"Of course. This afternoon." She frowned. "What's wrong? Don't you want to see him? Why ever not? He's very keen to see you. I'd say he worships you—exactly as if he were still five years old."

"They don't mature evenly," Prothero said.

"He hasn't forgotten a thing," she said.

In thickly falling snow, the Anderson boy jumped up and down on the little bridge and showed his teeth. He was still in the floppy Army surplus jacket. The clumsy Army surplus boots thudded on the planks. He took hold of the raw two by fours that were the railings of the bridge and tried to shake them with his big, clean hands. They didn't shake. Clumps of snow drifted under the bridge on the cold slow surface of the stream. Prothero stood on the bank, hands pushed into the pockets of the car coat. His ears were cold.

"It would hold a car." The Anderson boy came off the bridge. "If it was that wide. Not a nail in it. Only bolts and screws. No props in the stream-bed to wash out. Cantilevered."

Prothero nodded. "Good job," he said. "Your major will be engineering, then, right?"

"No." Half a head taller than Prothero, and very strong, the boy took Prothero's arm as if Prothero were old and frail, or as if he were a woman, and walked him back up the slope. "No, my grandfather's a contractor. I started working for him, summers, when I was fourteen. I got my growth early." He stopped on the flags and pawed at his hair to get the snow out of it. His hair was so white, it looked as if he were shedding.

"So you learned carpentry by doing?" Prothero reached for the latch of the sliding door to the den.

But the Anderson boy's arm was longer. He rolled the door back and with a hand between Prothero's shoulderblades pushed the man inside ahead of him. "It's like breathing or walking to me." He shut the door and helped Prothero off with his coat. "And just about as interesting." He took the coat to the bathroom off the den. He knew right where it was. Prothero watched him shed his own jacket there, and hang both coats over the bathtub to drip. He sat on the edge of the tub to take off his boots. "I wouldn't go to college to study it. I wouldn't do it for a living."

"What about coffee?" Barbara came into the den. He thought she looked younger. Maybe it was the new way she'd had her hair done. "It will be half an hour yet till dinner."

"I'll have coffee." The Anderson boy set his boots in the tub. He came out in a very white sweater and very white gym socks. His blue jeans were damp from the snow. He lifted bottles off the liquor cabinet and waved them at Barbara while he looked at Prothero with eyes clear as water, empty of intent as water. "Don will have a stiff drink."

"I'll have coffee," Prothero said, "thanks."

The Anderson boy raised his eyebrows, shrugged, and set the bottles down. Barbara went away. The Anderson boy dropped into Prothero's leather easy chair, stretched out his long legs, clasped his hands behind his head, and said, "No, my major will be psychology."

"That's a contrast," Prothero said. "Why?"

"I had a strange childhood," the Anderson boy

said. "My parents were murdered when I was five. But you knew that, right?"

Prothero knelt to set a match to crumpled newspaper and kindling in the fireplace. "Yes," he said.

"I didn't. Not till I was sixteen. My grandparents always claimed they'd been killed in a highway accident. Finally they thought I was old enough to be told what really happened. They were murdered. Somebody broke in at night. Into their bedroom. I was there—in the house, I mean. I must have heard it. Shouts. Screams. Gunshots. Only I blacked it all out."

"They said you went into shock." The kindling flared up. Prothero reached for a log and dropped it. His fingers had no strength. The Anderson boy jumped out of the chair, picked up the log, laid it on the fire. Sparks went up the chimney. He rattled the firescreen into place and brushed his hands.

"I stayed in shock," he said. "I couldn't remember it even after they told me. They showed me old snapshots—the house, my parents, myself. It still didn't mean anything. It was as if it was somebody else, not me."

"You wouldn't even talk." Prothero wanted not to have said that. He went to the liquor cabinet and poured himself a stiff drink. "It was on television. On the radio."

"Oh," Barbara said, coming in with mugs of coffee.

"I told you, didn't I?" the Anderson boy asked her.

"He's going to be a psychologist," Prothero said.

"I should think so," Barbara said, and took one of the mugs back to the kitchen with her.

The Anderson boy clutched the other one in both hands and blew steam off it. He was in the easy chair again. "I didn't utter a sound for weeks. Then they took me to a swim school. I was afraid of the water. I screamed. They had to call a doctor with a needle to make me stop."

Prothero blurted, "You could swim. I taught you."

The Anderson boy frowned. Cautiously he tried the coffee. He sucked in air with it, making a noise. He said, "Hey, that's true. Yeah, I remember now."

Prothero felt hollow. He drank. "Just like that?"

"Really. The pool—one of those little oval-shape ones. How the sun beat down out there—made you squint." He closed his eyes. "I can see you. What were you then—seventeen? Bright red swim trunks, no?"

Jean had given them to him. He'd been wearing floppy Hawaiian ones. The red ones were tight and skimpy. They'd made him shy but she teased him into wearing them. He felt her trembling hands on him now, peeling them off him in that glass-walled bedroom where the sun stung speckled through the loose weave of the curtains, and the Anderson boy napped across the breezeway. Prothero finished his drink.

The Anderson boy said, "And there was a big striped beach ball. Yeah." He opened his eyes and shook his head. "It's really fantastic, man. I mean, I can feel myself bobbing around in that water. I can taste the chlorine. And I won't go near a pool. They scare me to death."

"Every pool has chlorine and a beach ball." Prothero poured more whiskey on ice cubes that hadn't even begun to melt. "My trunks had to be some color."

"No, I swear, I remember. And that's why I came. When I saw you on TV, it began to happen. I began to remember—the house, the desert, my parents."

"The shouts?" Prothero asked numbly. "The screams? The gunshots?"

"Not that." The Anderson boy set down his mug. "I've read enough to know I'll probably never remember that." He pushed out of the chair and went to stand at the window. The light had gone murky. Only the snow fell white. "You can help me with the rest but you can't help me with that." He turned with a wan smile and held out his hands. "I mean, you weren't there. Were you?"

A shiny red moped stood under the thrust of roof above the front door. With the sunlight on the snow, it made the house look like a scene on Christmas morning. When the motor that let down the garage door stopped whining, Prothero heard the whine of a power saw from inside the house. The saw was missing from its hangers on the garage wall. He went indoors and smelled sawdust.

The Anderson boy was working in the den. He wasn't wearing a shirt. Barbara was watching him from the hall doorway. She smiled at Prothero. The noise of the saw was loud and she mouthed words to him and went off, probably to the kitchen. The Anderson boy switched off the saw, laid it on the carpet, rubbed a hand along the end of the eight inch board he'd cut and carried it to the panelled wall where pictures had hung this morning. He leaned it there with others of its kind and turned back and saw Prothero and smiled.

"Don't you ever have classes?" Prothero asked.

"I didn't get here in time to register," the Anderson boy said. "I'm auditing a little. I'll enroll for fall." He nudged one of the stacks of books on the floor. He was barefoot. "You need more shelves."

"I work in here, you know." The pictures were piled on the desk. He lifted one and laid it down. "I have lectures to prepare, papers to read, critiques to write."

"And books?" the Anderson boy said.

"No," Prothero said, "no more books."

"It was your book that led me to you," the Anderson boy said. "I owe a lot to that book."

Prothero looked at a photo of himself on a horse.

"I won't get in your way," the Anderson boy said. "I'll only be here when you're not." He looked over Prothero's shoulder. "Hey, you took me riding once, held me in front of you on the saddle. Remember?"

Barbara called something from the kitchen.

"That's lunch," the Anderson boy said, and flapped into his shirt. "Come on. Grilled ham and cheese on Swedish rye." He went down the hall on his big, clean, bare feet. He called back over his shoulder, "Guess whose favorite that is."

In the dark, Prothero said, "I'm sorry."

"You're still exhausted from that wretched tour." Barbara kissed him tenderly, stroked his face. "It's all right, darling. Don't brood. You need rest, that's all." She slipped out of bed and in the snow-lit room there was the ghostly flutter of a white nightgown. She came to him and laid folded pajamas in his hands. They were soft and smelled of some laundry product. "Sleep and don't worry. Worry's the worst thing for it."

He sat up and got into the pajamas. Buttoning them, he stared at the vague shape of the window. He was listening for the sound of the moped. It seemed always to be arriving or departing. The bed moved as Barbara slipped into it again. He lay down beside her softness and warmth and stared up into the darkness.

She said, "It's what all the magazine articles say."

"Who paid for the shelving?" he asked.

"You did," she said. "Naturally."

He said, "It's you I'm worried about."

"I'll be all right," she said. "I'll be fine."

The sound of the moped woke him. The red numerals of the clock read 5:18. It would be the man delivering the newspaper. He went back to sleep. But when he went out in his robe and pajamas to pick up the newspaper, he walked to the garage door. The moped had sheltered there, the new one, the Anderson boy's—the marks of the tire treads were crisp in the snow. There were the tracks of boots. He followed them along the side of the house. At the corner he stopped. He was terribly cold. The tracks went out to and came back from one of the clumps of birches on the lawn. Prothero went there, snow leaking into his slippers, numbing his feet. The snow was trampled under the birches. He stood on the trampled snow and looked at the house. Up there was the bedroom window.

In the new University Medical Center, he spent three hours naked in a paper garment that kept slipping off one shoulder and did nothing to keep from him the cold of the plastic chairs on which he spent so much of the time waiting. They were the same chairs in all the shiny rooms, bright colored, ruthlessly cheerful, hard and sterile like the walls, counters, cabinets, tables. Needles fed from the veins in his arms. He urinated into rows of bottles. A bald man sat in front of him on a stool and handled his genitals while he gazed out the wide and staring tenth floor window at the city under snow. The paper of his garment whispered to and mated with the paper on the examination table while his rectum was probed with indifferent ferocity. The X-ray table was high and hard, a steel catafalque. He feared the blocky baby-blue machine above it would snap the thick armatures that held it and drop it on him. The nurse need not have asked him to lie rigid. When he breathed in at her request, the sterilized air hissed at his clenched teeth. They told him there was nothing wrong with him.

"Do you remember the rattlesnake?" the Anderson boy asked. He had cut channels in the uprights and fitted the shelves into them. The workmanship was neat. Horizontals and verticals were perfect. He was staining the shelves dark walnut to match the others already in the den. The stain had a peculiar smell. Prothero thought it was hateful. The big blond boy squatted to tilt up the can of stain and soak the rag he was using. "We were always out there taking walks, hikes, weren't we? And one day there was this little fat snake."

"Sidewinder," Prothero said. "I thought you weren't going to be here when I was here."

"Sorry," the Anderson boy said. "I loused up the timing on this. Can't stop it in the middle. I'll be as fast about it as I can." He stood up and made the white of the raw fir plank vanish in darkness. "If you want to work, let me finish this half and I'll clear out."

"I was trying to teach you the names of the wildflowers. It would have been February. That's when they come out. Sidewinders don't grow big."

"It's a rattlesnake, though," the Anderson boy said. "Poisonous. I mean, you let me handle a nonpoisonous snake once. I can still feel how dry it was. Yellow and brown."

"Boyle's king snake." Prothero took off his coat.

"You remember what you did?" the Anderson boy said.

"About the sidewinder?" Prothero poured a drink.

"Caught it. Pinned it down with a forked stick back of its head. It was mad. It thrashed around. I can shut my eyes and see that. Like a film."

"I didn't want it sliding around with you out there. You could stumble on it again. If I'd been alone or with grownups I'd have just waited for it to go away."

The Anderson boy knelt again to soak the rag. "You had me empty your knapsack. You got it behind the head with your fist and dropped it in the sack. We took it to the little desert museum in town."

"There was nothing else to do," Prothero said.

"You could have killed it," the Anderson boy said.

"I can't kill anything," Prothero said.

"That's no longer accepted," the Anderson boy said. "Anybody can kill. We know that now. It just depends on the circumstances."

Kessler was on the University faculty, but he had a private practice. His office, in a new, one-story medical center built around an atrium, smelled of leather. It was panelled in dark woods. A Monet hung on one wall. Outside a window of diamond-shaped panes, pine branches held snow. From beyond a broad, glossy desk, Kessler studied Prothero with large, pained eyes in the face of a starved child.

"Has it ever happened to you before? I don't mean isolated instances—every man has those. I mean for prolonged periods, months, years."

"From the summer I turned eighteen until nearly the end of my senior year in college."

Kessler's eyebrows moved. "Those are normally the years of permanent erection. What happened?"

"I was having a crazy affair with, well, an older woman. In my home town. Older? What am I saying. She was probably about my age now."

"Married?" Kessler asked.

"Her husband traveled all the time."

"Except that once, when you thought he was traveling, he wasn't—right?" Kessler said.

"He caught us," Prothero said. "In bed together."

"Did you have a lot of girls before her?"

"None. Sexually you mean? None."

There were *netsuke* on the desk, little ivory carvings of deer, monkeys, dwarfish humans. Prothero thought that if it were his desk, he would be fingering them while he listened, while he talked. Kessler sat still. He said:

"Then she did the seducing, right?"

"We were on a charity fund-raising committee." Prothero made a face. "I mean, I was a token member, the high-school's fair-haired boy. The rest were adults. She kept arranging for her and me to work together."

"And after her husband caught you, you were impotent?"

"For a long while I didn't know it. I didn't care. I didn't want to think about sex." He smiled thinly. "To put it in today's parlance—I was turned off."

"Did the man beat you? Did he beat her?"

Prothero asked, "Why has it started again?"

"It's never happened in your married life?"

Prothero shook his head.

"How did you come to marry your wife? Let me guess—she was the seducer, right?"

"That's quite a word," Prothero said.

"Never mind the word," Kessler said. "You know what I mean. The aggressor, sexually. She took the initiative, she made the advances." His smile reminded Prothero of the high suicide rate among psychiatrists. Kessler said, "What do you want from me?"

"Yes," Prothero said. "She was the seducer."

"Has she lost interest in you sexually?"

"There's nothing to be interested in," Prothero said.

"Do you get letters from the woman?"

"What woman? Oh. No. No, she's—she's dead."

"On this book promotion tour of yours," Kessler said, "did you see the man somewhere?"

Prothero said, "I wonder if I could have a drink."

"Certainly." Kessler opened a cabinet under the Monet. Bottles glinted. He poured fingers of whiskey into squat glasses and handed one to Prothero. "Been drinking more than usual over this?"

Prothero nodded and swallowed the whiskey. It was expensive and strong. He thought that in a minute it would make him stop trembling. "They had a child," he said, "a little boy. I liked him. We spent a lot of time together. Lately, he saw me on television. And now he's here."

Kessler didn't drink. He held his glass. "What's your sexual drive like?" he asked. "How often do you and your wife have sexual relations?"

"Four times a week, five." Prothero stood up, looking at the cabinet. "Did."

"Help yourself," Kessler said. "How old is he?"

The trembling hadn't stopped. The bottle neck rattled on the glass. "Eighteen, I suppose. With his father away most of the time, he took to me."

"Does he look like his father?"

"It's not just that." Prothero drank. "He keeps hanging around. He's always at the house." He told Kessler about the footbridge, about the bookshelves. "But there's more. Now he comes at night on that damn motor bike and stands in the dark, staring up at our bedroom. While we're asleep."

"Maybe he's homosexual," Kessler said.

"No." Prothero poured whiskey into his glass again.

"How can you be sure?" Kessler gently took the bottle from him, capped it, set it back in place, and closed the cabinet. "It fits a common pattern."

"He's too easy with women—Barbara, anyway, my wife." Prothero stared gloomily into his whiskey. "Like it was her he'd known forever. They've even developed private jokes."

"Why not just tell him to go away?" Kessler asked.

"How can I?" Prothero swallowed the third drink. "What excuse can I give? I mean, he keeps doing me these kindnesses." Kessler didn't answer. He waited. Prothero felt his face grow hot. "Well, hell, I told him to keep out from under my feet. So what happens? He's there all the time I'm not. He's got changes of clothes in my closet. His shaving stuff is there. My bathroom stinks of his deodorant."

Kessler said, "Are they sleeping together?"

"Barbara and that child?"

"Why so appalled?" Kessler said mildly. "Weren't you a child when you slept with his mother?"

"Jesus." Prothero stood up.

"Don't go away mad," Kessler said. "You're going to get a bill for this visit, so you may as well listen to me. You're afraid of that boy. Now, why? Because he looks like his father—right? So what happened in that bedroom?"

"That was a long time ago." Prothero read his watch.

"Not so long ago it can't still make you impotent," Kessler said. "Thirty years old, perfect health, better than average sexual drive. It wasn't a beating, was it? It was something worse."

"It was embarrassing," Prothero said. "It was comic, wasn't it? Isn't that what those scenes always are? Funny?"

"You tell me," Kessler said.

Prothero set down the glass. "I have to go," he said.

When he stepped into the courtyard with its big Japanese pine, the Anderson boy was walking ahead of him out to the street. Prothero ran after him, caught his shoulder, turned him. "What are you doing here? Following me?"

The boy blinked, started to smile, then didn't. "I dropped a paper off on Dr. Lawrence. I've been sitting in on his lectures. He said he'd like to read what I've written about my case—the memory-loss."

Prothero drew breath. "Do you want a cup of coffee?"

"Why would you think I was following you?" The Anderson boy frowned at the hollow square of offices, the doors lettered with the names of specialists. "Are you feeling okay?"

"Nothing serious." Prothero smiled and clapped the boy's shoulder. "Come on. Coffee will warm us up."

"I have to get home. My grandparents will be phoning from California." He eyed the icy street. "I sure do miss that sunshine." His red moped was at the curb. He straddled it. Prothero couldn't seem to move. The boy called, "The shelves are finished. I'm going to lay down insulation in your attic next." He began to move off, rowing with his feet in clumsy boots. "You're losing expensive heat, wasting energy." The moped sputtered. If Prothero had been able to answer, he wouldn't have been heard. The Anderson boy lifted a goodbye hand, and the little machine wobbled off with him.

Prothero ran to his car and followed. The boy drove to the edge of town away from the campus, and turned in at an old motel, blue paint flaking off white stucco. Prothero circled the block and drove into an abandoned filling station opposite. The boy was awkwardly pushing the moped into a unit of the motel. The door closed. On it was the number nine. Prothero checked his watch and waited. It grew cold in the car, but it was past noon. The boy liked his meals. He would come out in search of food. He did. He drove off on the moped.

The woman behind the motel office counter was heavy-breasted, middle-aged, wore rimless glasses, and reminded Prothero of his own mother. He showed the woman his University I.D. and said that an emergency had arisen: he needed to get from Wayne Anderson's room telephone numbers for his family on the West Coast. The woman got a key and moved to come with him. But a gray, rumpled-faced man in a gray, rumpled suit arrived, wanting a room, and she put into Prothero's hand the key to unit nine. It needed new wallpaper, carpet, curtains, but the boy kept it neat. Except for the desk. The desk was strewn with notebook pages, scrawled with loose handwriting in ballpoint pen, with typewritten pages, with Xerox copies of newspaper clippings.

Dry-mouthed, he went through the clippings. They all reported the shootings and the aftermath of the shootings. The Anderson boy's mother had lain naked in the bed. The man had lain clothed on the floor beside the bed, gun in his hand. Both shot dead. The child had wandered dazedly in and out of the desert house, in sleepers, clutching a stuffed toy kangaroo, and unable to speak. Prothero shivered and pushed the clippings into a manila envelope on which the boy had printed CLIPPINGS. He picked up the notebook pages and tried to read. It wasn't clear to him what the boy had tried to do here. Events were broken down under headings with numbers and letters. It looked intricate and mad.

Prothero tried the typewritten pages. Neater, easier to read, they still seemed to go over and over the same obsessive points. No page was complete. These must be drafts of the pages the boy had taken to Dr. Lawrence. A red plastic wastebasket overflowed with crumpled pages. He took some of these out, flattened them, tried to read them, looking again and again at his watch. For an instant, the room darkened. He looked in alarm at the window. The woman from the motel office passed. Not the boy. Prothero would hear the moped. Anyway, he had plenty of time. But the crumpled pages told him nothing. He pushed them back into the wastebasket. Then he noticed the page sticking out of the typewriter. It read:

Don Prothero seems to have been a good friend to me,

*even though he was much older. My interviews with him
have revealed that we spent much time together. He taught
me to swim, though I afterward forgot how. He took me
on nature walks in the desert, which I also had forgotten
until meeting him again. He brought me gifts. The shock
of my parents' death made me forget what I witnessed that
night—if I witnessed anything. But why didn't Don come
to see me or try to help me, when he learned what had
happened? He admits he did not. And this is not consis-
tent with his previous behavior. My grandmother says he
did not attend the funeral. A friendship between a small
boy and a teenage boy is uncommon. Perhaps there never
was such a friendship. Maybe it wasn't me Don came to
see at all. Maybe he came—*

Prothero turned the typewriter platen, but the
rest of the page was blank. He laid the key with a
clatter on the motel office counter, muttered thanks
to the woman, and fled. His hands shook and were
slippery with sweat as he drove. He had a lecture
at two. How he would manage to deliver it, he
didn't know, but he drove to the campus. Habit got
him there. Habit would get him through the lecture.

Barbara's car was in the garage. He parked beside
it, closed the garage, went into the den, poured a
drink, and called her name. He wondered at the
stillness of the house. Snow began to fall outside.
"Barbara?" He searched for her downstairs. No-
where. She was never away at this hour. She would
have left a note. In the kitchen. Why, when she was
gone, did the kitchen always seem the emptiest of
rooms? He peered at the cross-stitched flowers of

the bulletin board by the kitchen door. There was no note. He frowned. He used the yellow kitchen wall phone. Cora answered, sounding perky.

He said, "Are you all right? Is Barbara there?"

"I'm fine. No—did she say she was coming here?"

"I thought there might have been an emergency."

"No emergency, Don. Every day, in every way, I'm—"

"I wonder where the hell she is," he said, and hung up. Of course, she wouldn't have been at her mother's. Her car was still here, and Cora wouldn't have picked her up—Cora no longer drove.

Had Barbara been taken ill herself? He ran up the stairs. She wasn't in the bathroom. She wasn't in the bedroom. What was in the bedroom was a toy kangaroo. The bedclothes were neatly folded back, and the toy kangaroo sat propped against a pillow, looking at him with empty glass eyes. Its gray cloth was soiled and faded, its stitching had come loose, one of the eyes hung by a thread. But it was the same one. He would know it anywhere. As he had known the boy.

"Christ," he whispered. He set the drink on the dresser and rolled open the closet. It echoed hollowly. Her clothes were gone. A set of matched luggage she had bought for their trip to Europe two years ago had stood on the shelf above. It didn't stand there now. Involuntarily, he sat on the bed. "But it wasn't my fault," he said. He fumbled with the bedside phone, whimpering, "It wasn't my fault, it wasn't my fault." From directory assistance he got the number of the motel. He had to dial twice before he got it right.

The motherly woman said, "He checked out. When I told him you'd been here, going through his papers, he packed up, paid his bill, asked where the nearest place was he could rent a car, and cleared right off."

"Car?" Prothero felt stupid. "What about his moped?"

"He asked me to hold it. He'll arrange for a college friend to sell it for him. Some boy. Goldberg?"

"Where is the nearest place? To rent a car, I mean."

"Econo. On Locust street. It's only two blocks."

The directory assistance operator didn't answer this time. Prothero ran down to the den. He used the phone book. The snow fell thicker outside the glass doors. He longed for it to cover the footbridge. Econo Car Rentals was slow in answering too. And when at last a dim female voice came on, he could not get it to tell him what he wanted to know.

"This is the college calling, don't you understand? He wasn't supposed to leave. His family are going to be very upset. There's been a little confusion, that's all. He can't be allowed to go off this way. Now, please—"

A man spoke. "What's this about Wayne Anderson?"

"He's a student," Prothero said. "Just a child. Do you realise he'll take that car clear out to California?"

"That information goes on the form. Routinely," the man said. "Are you a relative of this Wayne Anderson?"

"Ah," Prothero said, "you did rent him a car, then?"

"I never said that. I can't give out that kind of information. On the phone? What kind of company policy would that be?"

"If this turns out to be a kidnapping," Prothero said recklessly, "your company policy is going to get you into a lot of trouble. Now—what kind of car was it? What's the license number?"

"If it's a kidnapping," the man said, "the people to call are the police." His mouth left the phone. In an echoing room, he said to somebody, "It's some stupid college kid joker. Hang it up." And the phone hummed in Prothero's hand.

He was backing the car down the driveway when Helen Moore's new blue Subaru hatchback pulled into the driveway next door. He stopped and honked. She stopped too. The door of her garage opened. She didn't drive in. She got out of the car, wearing boots and a Russian fur hat. Before she closed the door behind her, Prothero glimpsed supermarket sacks on the seat. With a gloved hand, she held the dark fur collar of her coat closed at the throat. The door of her garage closed again. She came toward the snow-covered hedge. She blinked. Snowflakes were on her lashes. "Something wrong?"

"I'm missing one wife. Any suggestions?"

"Are you serious?" She tilted her head, worry lines between her brows. "You are. Don, dear—she left for the airport." Helen struggled to read her wristwatch, muffled in a fur coat cuff, the fur lining of a glove. "Oh, when? An hour ago? You mean you didn't know? What have we here? Scandal in academe?"

Prothero felt his face redden. "No, no, of course not. I forgot, that's all. Wayne Anderson came for her, right?"

"Yes. Brought her luggage out, put it in the trunk. Nice boy, that."

Prothero felt sick. "What did Barbara say?"

"She looked preoccupied. She was already in the car." She winced upward. "Can they really fly in this weather."

"There'll be a delay," Prothero said. "So maybe I can catch them. She's taking this trip for me. There are things I forgot to tell her. Did you notice the car?"

"Japanese. Like mine. Darling, I'm freezing." She hurried back to the Subaru and opened the door. "Only not blue, of course—I've got an exclusive on blue." Her voice came back to him cheerful as a child's at play in the falling snow. "White. White as a bridal gown." She got into the car and slammed the door. Her garage yawned again, and she drove inside.

Defroster and windshield wipers were no match for the snow. The snowplows hadn't got out here, yet. He hadn't put on chains, and the car kept slurring. So did others. Not many. Few drivers had been foolhardy enough to venture out of town. Those who had must have had life or death reasons. But life and death were no match for the snow, either. Their cars rested at angles in ditches, nosed in, backed in. The snow was so dense in its falling that it made blurs of the drivers' bundled shapes. They moved about their stranded machines like discoverers from some future ice age come upon the wreckage of our own.

A giant eighteen wheeler loomed through the whiteness. Prothero was on the wrong side of the road. He hadn't realized this. The truck came directly at him. He twisted the wheel, slammed down on the brake pedal. The car spun out of control— but also out of the path of the truck. He ended up, joltingly, against the trunk of a winter-stripped tree. He tried for a while to make the car back up, but the wheels only spun. He turned off the engine and leaned on the horn. Its sound was frail in the falling snow. He doubted anyone would hear it up on the empty road. And if the crews didn't find him before dark, they would stop searching. By morning, when they came out again, he might be frozen to death. There was a heater in the car, but it wouldn't run forever. He left the car, waded up to the road. He saw nothing, not the road itself, now, let alone a car, a human being. He shouted, but the thickly falling snow seemed to swallow up the sound. It was too far to try to walk back to town. Too cold. No visibility. He returned to the car. If he froze to death, did he care?

They found him before dark and delivered him, though not his car, back home. For a long time he sat dumbly in the den, staring at his reflection in the glass doors. Night fell. The doors became black mirrors.He switched on the desk lamp, reached for the telephone, drew his hand back. He couldn't call the police. Not now, any more than on that desert night twelve years ago. He got up and poured himself a drink. And remembered Goldberg. He got Goldberg's telephone number from admissions, rang it, left a message. He sat drinking, waiting for Goldberg to call. *Barbara,* he kept thinking, *Barbara.*

He heard the Anderson boy's moped. He had been asleep and the sound confused him. He got up stiffly and stumbled to the front door. The snow had stopped falling. The crystalline look of the night made him think it must be late. He read his watch. Eleven. He'd slept, all right. Even the snowplow passing hadn't wakened him. The street, in its spaced circles of lamplight, was cleared. He switched on the front door lamp. Goldberg came wading up the walk in a bulky windbreaker with a fake fur hood, his round, steel-rimmed glasses frosted over. He took these off when he stepped into the house. He had a round, innocent, freckled face. Prothero shut the door.

"Why didn't you phone?" he said.

The boy cast him a wretched, purblind look, and shook his head. "I couldn't tell you like that."

"Where is Anderson? Where did he tell you to send the money when you sold his moped?"

"Home. San Diego," Goldberg said. "Is that whiskey? Could I have some, please? I'm frozen stiff."

"Here." Prothero thrust out the glass. Goldberg pulled off a tattered driving glove and took the glass. His teeth chattered on the rim. Prothero said, "What was his reason for leaving? Did he tell you?"

Miserably, Goldberg nodded. He gulped the

whiskey, shut his eyes, shuddered. "Oh, God," he said softly, and rubbed the fragile looking spectacles awkwardly on a jacket sleeve, and hooked them in place. He looked at the door, the floor, the staircase—everywhere but at Prothero. Then he gulped the rest of the whiskey and blurted, "He ran off with your wife. Didn't he? I laughed when he said it. But it's true, isn't it? That's why you phoned me."

Prothero said, "My wife is in Mankato. Celebrating the birthday of an ancient aunt. I called you because I'm worried about Anderson."

"Oh, wow. What a relief." Goldberg's face cleared of its worry and guilt. "I knew he was a flake. I mean—I'm sorry, sir, but I mean, a little weird, right? I was a wimp to believe him. Forgive me?"

"Anything's possible," Prothero said.

"He really sold me." Goldberg set the empty whiskey glass on one of a pair of little gilt Venetian chairs beside the door. "See, I said, if he did it, I'd have to tell you. And he said I didn't need to bother—you'd already know." Goldberg pushed the freckled fat hand into its glove again. His child's face pursed in puzzlement. "That was kinky enough, but then he said something really spacey, okay? He said you wouldn't do anything about it. You wouldn't dare. What did he mean by that?"

"Some complicated private fantasy. Don't worry about it." Prothero opened the door, laid a hand on the boy's shoulder. "As you say, he's a little weird. Disturbed. And my wife's been kind to him."

"Right. He had a traumatic childhood. His parents were murdered. He told you, right?" Goldberg stepped out onto the snowy doorstep. "He said he liked coming here." Halfway down the path, Goldberg turned back. "You know, I read your book. It helped me. I mean, this is a killer world. Sometimes you don't think there's any future for it. Your book made me feel better." And he trudged bulkily away through the snow toward the moped that twinkled dimly in the lamplight at the curb.

Prothero shut the door and the telephone rang. He ran for the den, snatched up the receiver, shouted hello. For a moment, the sounds from the other end of the wire made no sense. Had some drunk at a party dialed a wrong number? No. He recognized Barbara's voice.

"Don't come," she shouted. "Don't come, Don."

And the Anderson boy's voice. "Apple Creek," he said. "You know where that is? The Restwell Motel." Prothero knew where Apple Creek was. West and south, maybe a hundred miles—surely no more. Why had he stopped there? The snow? But the roads would have been cleared by now. "We'll expect you in two hours."

"Let her go, Wayne. She had nothing to do with it."

"She has now. Don't worry. She's all right."

She didn't sound all right. In the background, she was screaming. Most of her words got lost. But some Prothero was able to make out. "He's got a gun. Don't come, Don. He'll kill you if you come."

"I'll be there, Wayne," Prothero said. "We'll talk. You've got it wrong. I'll explain everything. Don't hurt Barbara. She was always good to you."

"Not the way my mother was good to you."

Prothero felt cold. "You keep your hands off her."

"We're going to bed now, Don," the Anderson boy said. "That's all right. You just knock when you get here. Room eighteen. We won't be sleeping."

"Don't do this," Prothero shouted. "It was an accident, Wayne. I didn't kill them. I was only a kid."

But the Anderson boy had hung up.

The keys to Barbara's car ordinarily hung from a cup hook on the underside of a kitchen cupboard, but they weren't there now. He ran upstairs. She sometimes locked the keys inside her car. He was the professor, but she was the absent-minded one in the family. So she kept an extra set of keys. He fumbled through drawers with shaking hands, tossing flimsy garments out onto the floor in his panic.

He found the keys, started out of the bedroom, and saw the tattered toy kangaroo staring at him from the bed with its lopsided glass eyes that had seen everything. He snatched it up and flung it into a corner. He ran to it and drew back his foot to kick it. Instead, he dropped to his knees, picked it up, and hugged it hard against his chest and began to cry, inconsolably as a child. *Dear God, dear God!*

Blind with tears, wracked with sobs, he stumbled from the room, down the stairs, blundered into his warm coat, burst into the garage. When he backed down the drive, the car hard to control in the snow, twice wheeling stupidly backward into the hedge, the kangaroo lay face down on the seat beside him.

He passed the town square where the old courthouse loomed up dark beyond its tall, reaching, leafless trees, the cannon on the snow-covered lawn hunching like some shadow beast in a child's nightmare. No—the building was not entirely dark. Lights shone beyond windows at a corner where narrow stone steps went up to glass-paned doors gold-lettered POLICE. He halted the car at the night-empty intersection and stared long at those doors—as he had sat in his car, staring at the sunny desert police station on that long ago morning. *I was only a kid.* He gave a shudder, wiped his nose on his sleeve, and drove on.

The little towns were out there in the frozen night that curved over the snowy miles and miles of sleeping prairie, curved like a black ice dome in which the stars were frozen. Only the neon embroidery on their margins showed that the towns were there. At their hearts they were darkly asleep, except for here and there a streetlight, now and then a traffic signal winking orange. He had never felt so lonely in his life. He drove fast. The reflector signs bearing the names of the little lost towns went past in flickers too brief to read.

But there was no mistaking Apple Creek, no mistaking that this was the place he had headed for in the icy night, the end of his errand, the end of Don Prothero, the end so long postponed. The Restwell Motel stretched along the side of the highway behind a neat white rail fence and snow covered shrubs, the eaves of its snow-heaped roof outlined in red neon tubing.

And on its blacktop drive, not parked neatly on the bias in the painted slots provided by the management, but jammed in at random angles, stood cars with official seals on their doors, and with amber lights that winked and swivelled on their rooftops. Uniformed men in bulky leather coats, crash helmets, stetsons, boots, stood around, guns on their thighs in holsters, rifles in their gloved hands.

Prothero left his car and ran toward the men. The one he chose to speak to had a paunch. His face was red under a ten gallon hat. He was holding brown sheepskin gauntlets over his ears. He lowered them when he saw Prothero, but his expression was not welcoming.

Prothero asked, "What's happening here?"

"You want a room? Ask in the office." The officer pointed at a far off door, red neon spelling out OFFICE. But at that instant a clutch of officers on the far side of the bunched cars moved apart, and Prothero saw another door, the door they all seemed interested in. Without needing to, he read the numbers on the door. Eighteen.

"My wife's in there," he said.

The heavy man had turned away, hands to his cold ears again. But the brown wool hadn't deafened him. He turned back, saying, "What!" It was not a question.

"Barbara Prothero." He dug out his wallet to show identification cards. "I'm Donald Prothero."

"Hasenbein!" It was a name. The bulky man shouted it. "Hasenbein!" And Hasenbein separated himself from the other officers. He was twenty years younger than the bulky man. "This here's Lieutenant Hasenbein. You better tell him. He's in charge."

Hasenbein, blue-eyed, rosy-cheeked, looked too young to be in charge of anything. Prothero told him what seemed safe to tell. "He became a friend. He's disturbed."

"You better believe it," Hasenbein said. He dug from a jacket pocket a small black and white tube, uncapped it, rubbed it on his mouth like lipstick. "See that broken window?" He capped the tube and pushed it back into the pocket. "He fired a gun through that window."

"Oh, Christ," Prothero said.

"Why did he stop here, Doctor? Why did he telephone you? What does he want? Money?"

"There's something wrong with his mind," Prothero said. "He's got it into his head that I harmed him. He's trying to avenge himself. He phoned to tell me to come here. No, he doesn't want money. I don't know what he wants. To kill me, I guess. What brought you here?"

"The manager. He came out to turn off the signs. The switch box is down at this end. And he heard this woman screaming—your wife, right? In unit eighteen. He banged on the window and told them to quiet down or he'd call the Sheriff. And the kid shot at him. Luckily, he missed."

Prothero's knees gave. Hasenbein steadied him. "Is my wife all right?"

"There was only the one shot."

"There are so many of you," Prothero said. "Can't you go in there and get her out?" He waved his arms. "What's the good of standing around like this?"

"It's a question of nobody getting hurt needlessly."

"Needlessly! He could be doing anything in there. He could be doing anything to her. I tell you, he's out of his mind." Hasenbein didn't respond. He was too young. He was in way over his head. Prothero ran between the cars. "Barbara!" he shouted. "Barbara? It's Don. I'm here. Wayne? Wayne!" Two officers jumped him, held his arms. He struggled, shouting at the broken window, "Let her go, now. Let her come out. I'll come in and we'll talk. Just as I promised. I said I'd come, and I came. Do to me whatever you want. Shoot me, if you think that will solve anything. But let Barbara go. Wayne?"

No light showed beyond the broken window, but in the eerie, darting beams of the amber lights atop the patrol cars, Prothero saw for a moment what he took to be a face peering out. The Anderson boy said, "Tell them to let you go." Prothero looked at the officers holding him. They didn't loosen their grip on his arms. Hasenbein appeared. He twitched the corners of his boy mouth in what was meant for a reassuring smile and turned away.

"Anderson?" he shouted. "We can't do that. We can't let him come in there. We can't take a chance on what will happen to him. Why don't you calm down, now, and just toss that gun out here, and come out the door nice and quiet, with your hands in the air? We're not going to hurt you. That's a promise. It's a cold night, Anderson. Let's get this over with."

"Where's Barbara?" Prothero shouted. "What

have you done with her? If you've hurt her, I'll kill you."

"Sure," the Anderson boy shouted. Now his face was plain to see at the window. Prothero wondered why nobody shot him. "You killed my father and mother. Why not me? Why not finish off the whole family? Why didn't you kill me that night? Then there wouldn't have been any witnesses. Nothing but a toy kangaroo."

"I didn't kill them." Prothero gave his body a sudden twist. It surprised the men holding him. He got away. It surprised him too. He fell forward. The cold blacktop stung his hands. He scrambled to his feet and lunged at that broken window. He put his hands on the window frame and leaned into the dark room. "Your father came in from the breezeway. He was supposed to be out of town." Prothero heard his own voice shouting as if it were someone else's voice. He had cut his hands on the splinters of glass in the windowframe. He could feel the warm blood. He looked down. The blood steamed in the cold. "He had a gun, and he stood there in the doorway and shot at us. In the bed." Prothero was wondering why the Anderson boy didn't shoot him now. He was wondering what had happened to the officers. But he went right on. The words kept coming. "It was dark, but he knew where to shoot. I heard the bullet hit her. I heard it in my nightmares. For years and years. I rolled off the bed. He came at me, and I kicked him. In the crotch. And he bent over, and I tried to get past him, but he grabbed me. And I fought to get away. And the gun went off. You hear me, Wayne? He had the gun—not me. He shot himself—not me.

He shot himself. His blood got all over me, but I didn't kill him, I didn't kill him, I—"

"All right, Doctor." Hasenbein spoke almost tenderly. He took Prothero gently under the arms, straightened him, turned him. He frowned at Prothero's hands, swung toward the officers standing by the cars, the vapor of their breath gold in the flickering lights. "We need a first aid kit here." Hasenbein bent slightly toward the window. "Okay, Thomas—you can bring him out now."

"My wife," Prothero said. "Where's my wife?"

"Down at the substation, where it's warm," Hasenbein said. "She's all right. Scared, but all right."

A frail-looking officer with a mustache brought a white metal box with a red cross pasted to it. He knelt on the drive and opened the box. Carefully he took Prothero's bleeding hands. Prothero scarcely noticed. He stared at the door of unit eighteen. It opened and a police officer stepped out, followed by the Anderson boy in his shapeless Army fatigues and combat boots. He was handcuffed. Under his arm, a worn manila envelope trailed untidy strips of Xeroxed newspaper clippings. He looked peacefully at Prothero.

"What did you do to Barbara?" Prothero said.

"Nothing. You put her through this—not me. You could have told me any time." With his big, clean, carpenter's hands made awkward by the manacles, he gestured at the officers and cars. "Look at all the trouble you caused."

The Tango Bear

Stubbs used to do the cooking, but it had pained Hack Bohannon to watch him. Stubbs had been a rodeo rider in his time. Young, being sent flying from the backs of sunfishing broncos hadn't stopped him. Tramplings and tossings by brahma bulls were all in a dusty day's work—or play. But he had broken a lot of bones, some of them more than once. And time is on no man's side. By forty, he was no longer fit for the rodeo circuit. And he had left forty far behind him when he came to look after Bohannon's stables up Rodd canyon, above Madrone. He could still ride like part of the horse, if he could get into the saddle. But walking was another matter. After a few months, Bohannon had taken over the cooking.

He didn't mind. It was a way to get the day started. It gave point to getting out of bed. More than a year ago, now, Linda was taken hostage on a rotten tub of a fishing boat full of brown Mexican heroin, beaten, raped, half-drowned, and broken in her mind so that she no longer knew him or anyone else. At the time, Bohannon had loaded the Winchester to shoot himself. But he couldn't do it. If your stupidity brought harm to someone you loved, you lived with that. He went to bed sober, though he knew his dreams would likely be terrible. And he rose in the morning, though he knew the day would be little better. Having to cook helped.

A lean, dark man, shaggy-haired, an inch over six feet, and lately turned forty himself, he stood at a window of the pine plank kitchen, smoking, gazing out at the morning. The air that came in at the window was fresh, but the sky had a yellow tinge to it above the canyon trees and brush, which meant the day would be hot. And dry. When the hell was it going to rain? California canyons had a way of burning out. That was commoner down south. Here on the central coast, rains drifted in off the sea and regularly damped things down. In sheltered coves of these mountains, moss hung from the oaks. But this year rain was scarce. Bohannon dreaded a fire. He stabled a lot of horses—other peoples' horses, but he cared about them all, beautiful, ugly, gentle, mean. Big as they were, they were helpless. And horses were fools in fire.

The kettle shrieked, and he crossed from the window to pour boiling water into a big blue enamel coffee pot. He filled the kettle, set it back on the burner, and was folding biscuit dough, gazing up at one of Stubbs's horse drawings on the wall, when the old man's worn boot heels thumped the plank walkway that fronted the ranch house. The door banged open. Stubbs was in a shaving phase. Damp made his knuckles hurt, and in rain and fog he let his white whiskers sprout. But this morning, his jowls were smooth and pink. His eyes were a blue that must have wowed the girls in the old days. Now they were round with surprise and worry.

"You better come with me," he said.

"Don't tell me it's Lewis's colt again." Bohannon

sighed and rinsed the sticky dough off his hands. "I ought to charge them double for the nuisance." He pulled a shirt from a chairback and flapped into it. "What's he done this time?"

"It's no colt," Stubbs said. "It's a filly. She's pretty bunged up, too. Don't know how she got here, condition she's in." He hobbled away. Bohannon followed. "I never heard her. Rivera ought to heard her, but you know him. He sleeps the sleep of the blessed."

"What are you talking about?" Bohannon said.

"There's a girl in the empty box stall," Stubbs said.

There was. She lay asleep on fresh straw. Slender, young, about twenty, in jeans, blouse, fake suede zipper boots, floppy jacket—the kind of outfit girls at Madrone College wore. The clothes were torn and soiled. The girl's long, soft, dark hair had twigs and dry leaves tangled in it. Bohannon didn't like the way she was sleeping. He knelt and felt for a pulse. It was there, strong and regular. He saw blood on her other sleeve. He touched that sleeve and she gave a cry, opened her eyes, and cringed away from him.

"It's all right," he said. "We won't hurt you."

"Oh, God," she said, and pushed hair off her face. "I wanted to be gone by sunrise. I just couldn't walk any farther. I had to sleep." She tried to get to her feet, but the effort made her gasp. She went white and dropped to her knees. She put her good hand against the rough plank wall, planted a foot and tried to rise again. "I'll go on, now. I'm sorry for trespassing." The arm in the bloody sleeve hung limp. She managed a brief smile. "Could you"—her eyes begged—"just not tell anybody I was here?"

"You're hurt bad," Stubbs said. "Who done it to you?"

"I had an accident," she said. "Drove off the road."

He doubted it, but Bohannon was grateful for every word she spoke. When he'd found Linda this way, torn, bruised, bloody, aboard that filthy boat, she wouldn't speak a word. She would never speak again. She had gone to hide inside herself forever. "There's a phone in the house," he said. "We can call the Sheriff. Here, let me help you."

"No. Please, not the Sheriff."

"Come on." Bohannon reached for her. But she twisted half away and his hand struck the dangling arm. She gave a sharp cry, fell face forward in the straw, and lay still.

"Fainted," Stubbs said. "That arm looks broke."

Bohannon picked her up and carried her into the house.

Belle Hesseltine said, "I think you're making a mistake." She shut the hall door behind her, set her medical kit on a chair beside that door, and came to the long deal table where Stubbs, Rivera, and Bohannon were eating. Bohannon, mouth full, nodded, reached, dragged out a chair for her to sit on. She said, "You're borrowing trouble again. When are you going to learn?"

Bohannon swallowed and said, "Sit down. Try the eggs. They've got tomatoes and jalepenos in them. Those are sourdough biscuits. *Hecho a mano*. From scratch." With a smiling shake of her head for Bohannon's willfulness, the doctor sat. Bohannon said, "You know Stubbs. Rivera?"

Rivera was young, fragile looking, a seminarian aiming at the priesthood. But he worked hard, was good with the horses, and stronger than he looked. He gave the doctor a shy smile. Women frightened him. Stubbs ducked his head. "Ma'am," he said. Doctors frightened him.

"She's terrified," Belle Hesseltine told Bohannon. "She's in some kind of trouble, and it's far more serious than a few bruises and contusions." She flapped open a napkin and laid it in her lap. "Even than a broken arm."

"You don't know her? Never saw her before?"

"There are fifteen hundred students on that campus." Belle Hesseltine spooned eggs onto her plate, speared sausage links, took a biscuit from the basket. "And most of them are healthy the year around. No, I don't know her."

"No identification on her," Stubbs said. "Maybe she ain't a student. Maybe she don't come from around here."

"That jacket was bought at a shop in Madrone," Bohannon said. "It's on the label. The boots are from San Luis. She's from around here someplace." He gulped the last of his coffee, laid the napkin beside his plate, pushed back his chair. "She claims she drove off the road. If I find the car, it could tell me who she is." He got to his feet.

"She's lying about that," Belle Hesseltine said. "There is no car. Her injuries aren't that kind. I've treated a great many scrapes and bangs like hers. Those are hikers' injuries. She got those in a long, rough fall."

"People don't hike in the dark," Bohannon said.

"If it was only an accident"—Stubbs tilted back his chair and made a ragged cigarette—"what's she so scared of? Won't tell us her name. Don't want us to find her folks. We musn't call the law. Didn't even want us to call you. Just says, let her hide here till she's better. I guess she didn't fall. I guess somebody pushed her."

"I guess so," Bohannon said. "I want to know why. Before she gets better. I want to know who."

"Be careful, Hack," Belle Hesseltine said. "She seems a lovely, well-bred girl, but appearances can be so deceiving. You don't know what she's into, and who's in it with her. Drugs, prostitution? Let the Sheriff handle it."

Bohannon's laugh was sour. "If I hadn't let the Sheriff in on that Mexican heroin smuggling case, Linda might still be here." He bent and kissed the doctor's soft, old cheek. "Thanks for the house-call, Belle. And for keeping quiet about it."

"It's against my better judgment," she said strictly.

"I'll poke around, see what I can find." Bohannon went to the outer door. "I'll backtrack from the stables."

"It shouldn't take you long." The doctor rose abruptly from the table, making a face. Stubbs had lighted his cigarette. She waved away the smoke with a hand. "One of her ankles is badly sprained. She can't have come far." She gave Stubbs a severe look. "You're old enough to have better sense. Tobacco will kill you."

"I've been run over by a herd of buffalo," Stubbs said. "If that didn't kill me, I can stand a little smoke."

Bohannon went out into the bright sunlight.

She had come from farther than anyone with a sprained ankle should have been able to. Fear could sometimes mask out pain. He was winded and wet with sweat by the time he had climbed out of a ravine of big old oaks to this ragged blacktop road. Gazing around at the brown slopes and ridges, he did some mental mapwork. After rolling and ricocheting down this hundred foot drop, she'd blundered through the dark a good five miles. The drop here was steep. He'd had to haul himself up by grabbing chaparral and rock, his clothes were torn now like hers, his hands bleeding the same way.

He stood, panting, looking up and down the road. A few yards along, black streaks of fresh rubber lay on the pitted asphalt that sun and rain had bleached to gray. Somebody had stopped a car there. He walked down for a closer look. That car had been going far too fast for such a twisting road. It had also stopped too fast, skidded a long way, swerving wildly, damn near out of control. He gauged it was a big car, heavy, the tires new.

In the morning stillness, the sound reached him now of another car coming. He stepped onto the road shoulder. The car came around a bluff where a gnarled pine leaned out above the road. The car was taking its time. It wasn't a car he recognized— beige, two-three years old, compact, anonymous. He didn't recognize the driver, either. Ranch hat with a curled-up brim, little neckerchief, open collar, whipcord jacket, everything tan. Bohannon gave him a neighborly nod and lift of the hand. The man drove past. If he saw Bohannon it was from behind wrap-around sunglasses. He probably didn't see Bohannon. He was looking at the landscape. The landscape here was worth looking at.

Bohannon stepped into the road and crouched. Between last night's skidmarks, where they ended, lay a spot of oil. Fresh, no dust on it. He chewed his lower lip. Funny. The car must have stood here for a time. What the hell for? He straightened, knees giving small cracks that said he was too old for this, and walked back along the road. Dry brush edged the blacktop, knee-high. Many yards back, just about even with the place where the tire tracks began, right at the spot where Bohannon judged the girl had tumbled into the ravine, the brush was smashed flat. He knelt and examined it. A swatch of calico caught his eye—the fabric of the girl's shirt. He unsnagged it and pushed it into a pocket with the other bits he'd found along her trail, a drawstring from her jacket, a decorative bootstrap.

Out of the pocket he drew a V-shaped rag of tweed. He blinked at it in his fingers. He lifted his eyes and looked back along the road to where the car had stopped and unaccountably waited. The girl had worn no tweed, but Bohannon had found this caught on a fallen oak branch down below. So, had the driver of the car worn tweed, left the car, clambered down after her? It looked like it. Why? Had he tried to kill her by pushing her out of the car as it tore along through the night? Had he left the car and followed to make sure she was really dead? Or had she jumped from the car, and had he followed to fetch her back? He'd failed. Her fear had outrun his purpose, whatever it was. Bohannon frowned at the scrap, fingered it. Good tweed, hand-loomed. Expensive. He gave his head a shake, pushed the bit of wool back into his pocket, and headed for home, wishing for a horse.

When he got back to the place, kids on horses came swaying out the gate, saddle leather creaking. Stubbs helped two small children ride slowly around the paddock. A young couple from Los Osos wanted boarding and exercise rates—they were leaving on a cruise. In the shadows of the stable, Rivera helped the blacksmith from over in Paso Robles. It seemed an ordinary day. As Bohannon showered, he saw out the bathroom window horses grazing the long pastures that sloped up to the sunburned mountains, horses standing sleepily together in the shadows of oaks. A peaceful scene. What was a frightened girl doing in the middle of it?

While he heated soup for her, he built her a thick beef and cheese sandwich, and poured a glass of milk. Carrying bowl, sandwich, milk on a tray, he rapped the door of the room where they'd put her. She made a sleepy sound that he took to be permission to enter. She moved drowsily under a patchwork quilt on an old pine poster bed. Blinking, trying to smile, pushing hair off her face, which was badly scraped down one side, she sat up. The broken arm was in a neat sling. Bohannon set the tray on the bedside table, and arranged pillows for her so she could manage the tray on her lap.

"I'll repay you for all this," she said solemnly.

"All right." He dragged a chair to the bedside, sat down, put his hands on his knees, and told her what he had done with his morning. "After you jumped out of the car, he stopped it and tried to follow you. It was too dark, and he gave up. But only for the time being—right?"

She ate with the hunger of the healthy young, spooning up the thick, home-made soup. She gave him a quick glance. "This is good. Thank you. I was starving. But I won't stay and eat you out of house and home. I'll be on my way, now."

"Not on that ankle. On your way where?"

"It's not your worry." She took a big bite of the sandwich, chewed a while, washed the bite down with a long gulp of milk. "Someplace far away."

"You didn't bring any money," he said.

"I'll be all right. You've done all you could." She finished off the soup. "Lucky for me I stumbled on your place. There aren't that many kind people left in the world."

"That sounds grownup," Bohannon said, "but not calling the law when someone's trying to kill you— that doesn't."

"Kill me?" She opened her eyes wide, mocking him.

"Rape you, then," Bohannon said.

She stared. Color crept into her face. "What?" Her laugh was brief and sad. "Rape? Oh, no." She frowned. "You ask questions like a policeman." She looked out the window. "But you're not. You're a rancher. Horses."

"I was a deputy sheriff for fourteen years," he said. "Just about long enough to learn that people only jump from speeding vehicles for very serious reasons."

She bit her lip to keep from smiling. Her eyes never smiled. "He won't find me here."

"He knows the kind of fall you had, knows you had to be hurt and couldn't go far. There's a seminary over that ridge." He lifted an arm to point. "There's Ludlow's apple ranch down Sills canyon. And there's here. Not many places to have to search. And he's searching, isn't he?"

"I said I'd go." She glared at him, picked up the tray, pushed it into his hands. "Thank you for the meal. And for the doctor. And the wash and the sleep. But I don't want to put you in any danger." She flung back the bedclothes. Belle had put her into an old pair of his pajamas, cuffs rolled up on the pants and one sleeve, the other sleeve hanging because of the sling. She swung her legs over the bedside and tried to stand. "Oh, wow," she whispered, and went white, and sat down hard.

"I'm not in any danger." Bohannon set the tray on the floor and helped her lie back against the pillows again. He pulled the quilt up over her. "But you are. Tell me his name, and what this is all about. I can help you."

She lay with her eyes shut. She shook her head. "No. That's where you're wrong. You're sweet, but you're wrong." She opened her eyes. She was very earnest. "There are things that happen to us that no one can help us with. It's a big world, with billions of people in it, but some of them are all alone, and always will be." She closed her eyes again, and two tears ran down her face.

"I don't understand," Bohannon said. "The man terrifies you, yet you're protecting him."

"You do understand," she said, and was asleep.

Bohannon picked up the tray and softly left the room.

What kind of magazines would she like? The rack in the cool arcade of boutiques off the sunny main street in San Luis appeared to have every kind there was. She didn't seem to him the *Good Housekeeping* sort. He chose *The New Yorker, Los Angeles,* and one called *Ms.* Television reception was bad at his place because of the surrounding mountains, and cable hadn't come in yet. Reading would help her pass the time.

Magazines under his arm, he went along the shadowy corridor to a lively high-countered place that made fancy sandwiches and had Anchor steam beer on draft. It was great beer. He carried a tall cold glass of it out into the sunshine and sat by a rocky stream there to drink it among noisy college youngsters. He smoked cigarettes and let time slide because he hated going to the sheriff's station.

But after a second beer, he made himself go. A good many men in sand-color uniforms spoke his name in the halls, and he spoke theirs. But he felt more out of place here now than any stranger. He ended up in an office that had once been his—before he had resigned over the whitewash of an officer who in cold blood had shot down an unarmed Latino kid. Gerard sat at a desk still piled with too much work for one man to handle.

Gerard didn't smile at Bohannon, and Bohannon would never in his life again smile at Gerard. But Gerard got Bohannon the missing person file without comment, without question. He knew better than to ask Bohannon to sit down, and Bohannon remained standing to leaf through the file. People kept wandering off, but none of them on any of these sheets remotely resembled the sad, frightened girl in his spare bedroom. He handed the file back with thanks, and walked out of the station as quickly as he could. To him, it smelled of death.

The attendance office of the sprawling new Madrone Community College smelled only of fresh paint. But the woman in charge simply smiled disbelief when Bohannon asked about absent female students, and passed over the counter to her a drawing of the girl he'd had Stubbs make from memory. Stubbs was best at horses, but he could draw a good human likeness when he put his mind to it and his knuckles didn't hurt too much. The woman set reading glasses on her beaky nose, examined the drawing, handed it back. She pulled the glasses down and looked at him over them. "I'm sorry. She might be almost anyone." Bohannon had to agree. Crossing the campus to get here, he had passed at least a dozen.

He drove north from the college toward the town, a clutch of spindly Victorian frame houses on sleepy, narrow streets. Behind it, livestock grazed foothills. Farther back, the mountains rose. To the west, hills forested by tall pines blocked out sight of the ocean, scarcely a mile away. The town was trying to wake up. Fresh paint had been laid on the jigsaw work and turrets of the old houses— wedding cake tints. On the main street, shopfronts had been rusticated with planks to look like a set decorator's notion of the Olde West. He didn't care for that. Tourists were supposed to. So far, not many had—dogs still slept in the middle of main street. Bohannon only came here for the shop that sold coffee beans.

Outside town, in a meadow with a little stand of pines at the lower end, where rumor had it a new shopping center was going to be built someday soon, he was surprised to find tents pitched, a ferris wheel and other shiny rides set up, a faded canvas midway with games of chance and hot dog stands—a traveling carnival. Metallic music reached him in the pickup as he passed. He saw loud-speaker horns on tall barber-striped poles that held strings of lightbulbs and plastic pennons, red, blue, yellow, green, that fluttered in the wind. He shook his head. He couldn't recall a carnival ever stopping in Madrone before. He drove on to the coffee bean place.

The sun was setting behind his own hills when he got back to the stables and ranch house in Rodd canyon, braked the pickup in a swirl of dust, and climbed down out of it with the magazines and sacks of coffee beans. He slammed the tinny cab door and made for the kitchen, where Stubbs was at the stove, pushing food around in a big skillet. The old man had a clock in his head. Things had to happen on time. It was good for the business—horses thought the same way. Supper time was supper time. Bohannon set down his burden and went to the stove for a look. Stubbs glanced at him. "Turkey hash. All right with you?"

"Smells good," Bohannon said.

"You know a fella named Williams?" Stubbs asked.

"No. What about him?" Bohannon found a tumbler in a cupboard, ice cubes in a lumbering old refrigerator. "Did he come here? What for?"

"Said he'd like to buy your spread." Stubbs salted

the hash from a big tin shaker. "He looked the stables over, nail by nail. Squinted into every corner. Not too easy for him, either. Walks with them aluminum crutches that clamp around your arms? Short legs, all bent out of shape. Worse off than me."

Bohannon took the glass of ice and a bottle of Old Crow to the table. The table was neatly set. As always when Stubbs cooked, a big jug of ketchup stood in the middle. Bohannon sat down and poured himself a drink. "It's not for sale. Why did you let him waste his time?"

"He don't know the meaning of 'not for sale'."

Bohannon tasted the whiskey and lit a cigarette. "You been keeping an eye on the girl? Did you ask her if she likes turkey hash?"

"She's mostly been asleep," Stubbs said. "Them painkillers do that to you. Found her once, trying to get to the bathroom. That's a mighty tender ankle. I expect she's sore pretty much all over. Way I remember it. Be worse tomorrow. Poor little thing. I carried her to and fro."

"Keep that up," Bohannon said, "and you'll be down in bed, yourself."

"Williams wanted to look through the house," Stubbs said. "I told him he'd have to ask you. Acted like he didn't hear. Headed straight for it, hauled himself up on the porch, started peeking in the windows."

"It was a beige compact, right?" Bohannon said. "He wore wrap-around sunglasses, a little neckerchief, cowboy hat with the brim crimped up on the sides?"

"You do know him," Stubbs said.

"He doesn't want to buy this place," Bohannon said. "He's looking for the girl. I saw him this morning."

"I run him off." Stubbs limped to the kitchen door, pushed open the screen, leaned out, and whistled for Rivera. He let the screen fall shut and frowned at Bohannon. "You think he's the one that tried to kill her?"

"And so do you," Bohannon said. "You didn't say anything to her about him, I hope."

Stubbs shook his head. "I'm smarter than I look. I figured she'd try to run away, and she ain't ready for that." He rattled plates down out of a cupboard. "I thought you said it was a heavy car."

"A man can change cars." Bohannon worked on his drink. "Did you get the license number?"

"Covered with mud," Stubbs said. "Neat. Like it was laid on with a paintbrush. And I don't see like I used to."

"Probably a rental car," Bohannon said, "and if we checked, it wouldn't be any Williams anybody ever knew."

Rivera came in with his hair slicked down by water.

Bohannon awoke in pitch darkness. That was wrong. Ground lights glowed outside all night. Up in the meadows, horses were running hard, nickering, afraid. In the stables, horses snorted fear, hoofs kicked walls. Bohannon left the bed so fast he fell. He groped for the Winchester by the dresser where it always stood. But tonight Rivera had it. Bohannon had posted him on a kitchen chair on the porch outside the girl's room to guard her. Bohannon poked into a shirt, yanked on pants, leaned out the window. "Rivera?" He couldn't see. He tried the lightswitch. No light. A power outage? They were common enough in storms, but tonight was calm and clear. "Rivera?" Bohannon climbed out the window onto the porch. He could hear Stubbs cussing out the horses in the stables. Bohannon didn't head that way. He ran along the planks to the girl's room. The chair was there—he stumbled over it. But the man he fell against was not Rivera. This was a thick man with a bad smell to him.

"What's the matter?" It was the girl's voice, thin.

"Stay down," Bohannon shouted. The man struggled. Bohannon got a knee in the mouth. He tried for a better grip, and the man twisted away from him. Bohannon, on hands and knees, saw the man above him, silhouetted against faint starlight. The man raised the rifle and swung it down. Bohannon ducked, but the stock struck his shoulder, and he heard bone crack. He lay on his face and for a moment knew only pain, no sight, no sound, no thought. Then he heard the man running away. Groaning, Bohannon struggled to his feet. He clutched a porch post. "Catch him, Rivera," he shouted. "Catch him, Stubbs." He reeled off the porch and tried to run.

The girl called from the window. "What is it?"

"Horse thief," Bohannon lied. "Happens all the time." The motor of a large vehicle thrashed to life out in the road. Headlights went on out there. Gears clashed, a hulking, dark shape lurched down the trail. Shaggy eucalyptus trees edged the property there. He couldn't see well, but damned if the thing didn't look like a horse van. He opened his mouth to shout at it, but no sound came. He collapsed in the dust.

He awoke in his bed with his arm bound tight across his ribs, and sun pouring in the window. Stubbs stood beside the bed with a tray of food. He grinned. "Belle Hesseltine says if you mixed that shot she give you with whiskey you'd sleep forever." Bohannon numbly blinked and yawned. The memory came back vaguely of gaunt, grim Belle, by the soft light of a kerosene lamp, setting his collar bone at three in the morning, and saying sternly, "I told you so, and I'm not ashamed to say it. Now, you put that girl in the Sheriff's hands. That man could have shot you dead."

Bohannon said, "He didn't come to shoot."

"Can you sit up?" Stubbs said. "You want help?"

Bohannon shook his head, pushed himself into position with his right arm. "What time is it?"

"Noon." Stubbs set the tray on Bohannon's knees. "Been all quiet and regular so far." He sat down. "Them's poached eggs. Invalid food."

"Did the girl believe me about the horse thief?"

"I looked in twice. All she does is sleep."

"Good." Bohannon ate for a moment in silence, frowning. He blinked at Stubbs. "What upset the horses? They don't pay any attention to the lights going out."

"Not as a rule," Stubbs said. "Power company come and fixed the line an hour ago. Cut, all right. Deliberate."

"He meant to take the girl," Bohannon said.

"So it was smart to stir up the horses," Stubbs said. "Rivera run off to see what was bothering them. He's ashamed of himself, feels like he let you down bad. Specially about the rifle—leaving the rifle behind for that bastard."

Bohannon made to shrug and felt pain. "Rivera didn't want the rifle from the start. Priests don't shoot people. It was natural for him to forget it."

"I didn't take the horses acting up for what it was." Stubbs shook his head sadly. "A diversion. If I'd of had my wits about me, I'd have come direct to help the girl."

"You did right." Bohannon drank coffee. Stubbs had ground some of the new beans. The coffee was fine. "But I still don't know what got into them." He pointed. "You want to light me a cigarette, please? They're in my shirt."

Stubbs got cigarette pack and matches from the shirt, lit a cigarette and gave it to Bohannon, wrinkled his nose, turned back, picked up the shirt and smelled it. "Well, I'll be," he said mildly. "Bear." He dropped the shirt.

Bohannon stared at him through smoke. "Bear?"

"That's what scared the horses," Stubbs said. "Never thought I'd get a whiff of bear again. Last time was in Wyoming, nineteen and twenty eight. I was working cattle for a fella by the name of—"

"It was on his clothes," Bohannon said. "Rank. I remember wondering how any man could smell like that."

"Beats me," Stubbs said. "You and me smell like horse a lot of the time, but we live with horses. Nobody lives with a bear."

"The carnival," Bohannon said.

But he didn't go there. Dressed, a little stupified by the drug Belle had shot him full of, but able to navigate on his feet, and ready to drive the pickup, he was halfway to it, jingling the keys, when he remembered what Stubbs had said about the girl. He went back inside, rapped her door, waited, opened the door. A shape was under the patchwork quilt, all right. But it wasn't her shape. He knew it before he threw the quilt back. She had laid pillows underneath.

Her boots had stood on the shiny broad floorboards beside the chest of drawers. They were gone. Stubbs had washed her clothes and laid them in a drawer. He pulled the drawer open. Nothing. He left the room, wondering how much of a head start she had on him. Only one answer made sense. She had left as soon as she could after the man had left—the man who smelled like a bear. She had fled in panic. He couldn't blame her. But chancy as his protection had proved, she was worse off on her own. He had to bring her back.

He chose a gray gelding called Seashell. He wouldn't shy at a clumsy mounting, and he was sure-footed, and Bohannon believed the girl would keep away from roads and not seek a place full of people this time. He'd have to look for her where there weren't always trails. Watching Rivera saddle the gray, Bohannon disliked himself for wishing the girl pain. But he hoped that ankle was making travel slow for her. He hoped Stubbs's memory of how her kind of bruises felt two days afterward was right. Rivera held Seashell's head while Bohannon used a child's mounting block to crawl awkwardly into the saddle.

"Don't get down," Rivera said. "You can't get back up."

Bohannon found her trail nearby, but soon lost it. He crossed and recrossed ridges, firebreaks, circled clumps of oak, waded through chaparral, traced barrancas, most of them dry, one with a little trickle of a creek rambling down it. And here was a place where she had stopped to rest. She had knelt to drink from the creek. Her limp showed plainly in the indentations of her boots in the sand here. But she had left the sand before long. Lunging, Seashell got Bohannon up out of the barranca.

The sun was going down. He was in Sills canyon, and ready to give up. It was too far. He had missed her somehow back along the track. He was weary from the saddle, and the ache in his shoulder was strong. He wanted a drink, a hot bath, a meal, and sleep. He reined the patient gray around, and headed homeward by a trail he hadn't taken. After a mile or two, he sighted the burnt-out cabin. The chimney stood, three walls, a section of roof. Burnt out so long ago he couldn't recollect when. He eased Seashell down there. And before he reached the yard, he heard her weeping. Brush crackling under the horse's hoofs, Bohannon walked him close and looked inside. She was huddled on the hearth.

"Aren't you hungry?" he said. "You didn't bring food."

She nodded mutely, wiping her nose on her jacket sleeve, like a little kid. Sobs still jerked her when she pushed up off the hearth and came forlornly hopping through the trash, bottles, cans on the floor. She held onto a charred upright and gazed at him. He slid down from the horse—it was almost a fall. He held out the reins to her.

"I never rode a horse," she said.

"I'll lead him, then," Bohannon said. "You just sit in the saddle, all right? Come on, I'll help you up."

"I can't sleep in that room again," she said.

"They won't be back," he said. "I'm going after them."

She stared. "You don't know who they are."

"I know who one is," he said. "That's a start."

"I didn't tell you," she said. "Please remember that."

The dusty bulbs strung on frayed and sagging wires from the striped poles lit the tent tops now, and made of the carnival an island of hectic brightness in the night. The fast rides whirled, their gaudy red, blue, gold metal pods gleaming and glinting, children hanging on white-knuckled, trailing shrieks of joy and terror. The ferris wheel rose sedate against the stars, the wheel strung with tiny lights that were like stars themselves, the seats of the wheel swinging grandmotherly as rocking chairs. The faces of the riders were pale ovals in the fairytale glow.

He climbed stiffly down from the pickup onto the trampled grass of the meadow, among disorderly rows of newer pickups, campers, family cars, and heard the wheeze of an orgatron, the thin clash of its cymbals, the rattle of its snare drum. Walking past the noisy, hulking generator trucks, he smiled when he sighted a miniature merry-go-round, all carved and gilded and aglitter with mirrors, the small horses all curly manes and tails and flared nostrils, rising and sinking on their shiny poles, carrying cowboys three, four, five years old, wide-eyed with wonder.

The midway was crowded with high school and college youngsters, loud and rollicking, munching tacos and hotdogs, guzzling soft drinks from cans. Some of them tried hard to look superior and bored—a carnival was corny, after all, strictly hicktown. But Bohannon judged most of them had never had a crack at one before, and would remember it forever, no matter what they pretended. The canvas caves of yellow light that held the baseball throws, the rifle shoots, the wheel of fortune, were doing business just as brisk as the one where a battery of new electronic games beeped and twittered.

At the end of the midway—it wasn't a long walk—the circular show tent loomed up behind a limp facade of weathered canvas posters. The smell of animals was strong here on the cool night air, the smells of tanbark and crackerjack. Bohannon looked at the crackled paintings of llamas, zebras, seals. Trick dogs wore tiny clown hats and tutus. Young men in white hung upside down from trapezes. A pretty young lady walked a tightwire. Two young blacks on tall unicycles played basketball. And here was what he had come for. THE TANGO BEAR. The sign painter had made the bear about ten feet tall and snarling. *See him dance. See him rollerskate. See him ride a motorcycle.*

The window of the truck from which tickets were

sold was closed. Bohannon knocked on it. No one opened it. He made his way around to the back of the tent. A good many of what you might mistake for horse vans stood here in the near darkness. Their doors hung open, though. The animals were behind the canvas at his back. He could hear them shift and breathe and munch. A hoof clattered a bucket. Bohannon dropped to his knees and lifted the tent flap to peer inside. He wasn't looking for hoofs, flippers, paws. He hoped to see human feet. And he did—in manure-crusted work shoes.

A freckled, red-haired girl in dirty jeans and a flannel shirt too big for her, the tails almost to her knees, looked down at him. "Aren't you a little old for sneaking in?" She had the voice of a very tough small boy. "Buy a ticket."

"Nobody will sell me one." Bohannon worked himself under the canvas, gripped a pole, pulled himself to his feet. A fat zebra kicked backward at him. He jumped aside. "Where do I find the Tango Bear?"

"Last sighted parked up by Hearst Beach," she said. "He missed both daytime shows. If he doesn't get back here"—she glanced at a wristwatch—"in twenty-five minutes, Mr. Cathcart will probably kill him. Not the bear. Pancho, I mean. What is it about Pancho?" The girl regarded Bohannon's bad arm. "Only handicapped people want to see him."

"You mean Williams? Aluminum crutches?"

"That's the one." A taffy-colored llama nosed the girl's butt. She gave its muzzle a slap. "Gertrude, I told you, no more carrots." But Gertrude was not taking no for an answer, and the girl moved her pockets out of the llama's reach. "Williams scares Pancho. Are you going to scare him too?"

"He borrowed something of mine last night," Bohannon said. "I'd like to have it back. I'll be around for a while. Don't tell him I'm looking for him." He offered her a twenty dollar bill. She shook her head. He put the money away. "I want it to be a surprise," he said.

"Williams is coming tonight," she said. "That's why I told Mr. Cathcart not to worry about Pancho turning up for the evening show. Pancho won't cross Williams."

"You're a psychologist," Bohannon said.

She shrugged. "I live with animals." She reached into the loose shirt and brought out a tiny monkey. It scampered up her arm to perch on her shoulder, lean against her ear, peer anxiously at Bohannon, and squeak. The girl said, "After a while, you figure them out, and people are no different."

The fat zebra kicked at Bohannon again.

"Except meaner," the girl said.

Bohannon sat on the grass with his back against the vibrating wheel of one of the mobil generators. He was in shadow, and he could watch the highway from here. Laughter and shouts came from the midway, the rides. The merry-go-round music wheezed. Cars and pickups and RVs arrived and departed from the parking area. He watched for the beige compact. Maybe a large car too, expensive. And he watched for the van that held the Tango Bear. A voice crackled through the trumpet-shaped metal loudspeakers up the poles.

"Hur-ry, hur-ry, hur-ry. The big show is about to begin in the main tent. Get your tick-ets now, folks." The voice was a rasp, the words a drone.

"Thrills, spills, chills. Ac-ro-bats, clowns, wild ani-mals, death defying trap-eze acts. Perform-ing poo-dles from Par-ee. Won-der-ful trained seals. See the two-ton Tango Bear. He'll dance for you. This isn't TV, folks. This is all real, hap-pen-ing live before your ve-ry eyes. Don't miss it. You'll never for-give yourself. The ticket office is now open at the end of the mid-way. Hur-ry, hur-ry, hur-ry. Get your tick-ets now . . ."

The background of the highway as he viewed it was thick pine wood climbing slopes. Dark. Out of the darkness loomed the van, and lumbered along toward the big tent. Bohannon rose and watched. Lettering showed up on the side of the truck as it came into the light. THE TANGO BEAR. Bohan-non started for the midway. The voice blared on from the loudspeakers. "Hur-ry, hur-ry, hur-ry." He took the advice, pressing through the crowd, trying not to jar his sore shoulder, and not always avoiding it. He wanted to reach Pancho before the man was joined by his two-ton, ten-foot-tall friend.

He jammed for a minute in the crowd around the ticket truck. He was told to watch who he was shoving, and was himself shoved. He tripped over a tent stake and sprawled. Pain from his shoulder immobilized him for a moment. Then he used a bristly guy rope to haul himself to his feet. And in that instant, he glimpsed Williams in a seersucker suit at the far end of the midway. He was hobbling toward Bohannon as fast as he could on his shiny crutches. Bohannon wanted to talk to him, but he'd better get to Pancho first. He jogged around the tent to where the animal vans stood in the dark.

The rear doors of the Tango Bear truck were not open like the rest. He banged on them. The bear grunted and shuffled inside. Bohannon looked into the cab of the van. No Pancho. A tent flap let out a triangle of light. He stepped inside. The freckle-faced girl was in spangled white costume now, a tiara in her red hair. She didn't look the same. Her fairy godmother had been here. Bohannon envied the prince. The girl had blanketed the llamas in red and blue velvet with rhinestones, and crowned the zebras with silver and black plumes. She blinked sparkly false eyelashes at Bohannon.

"I heard Pancho's truck," she said. "Where is he?"

"That's what I was going to ask you," Bohannon said.

"Go find him," she said, "and tell him to get in here."

"Maybe he's with Williams," Bohannon said, and went out into the dark.

But now he had lost Williams. Williams hadn't joined the friendly folk around the window of the ticket truck. Bohannon started up the midway, eyeing the dwindling crowd. Williams wasn't pitching baseballs, throwing darts, or buying chances on a number on the big wheel. He wasn't frowning in concentration at the controls of an electronic game, nor among the jumping kids at the high, hot, greasy counters of the food trucks. Bohannon cut around behind the rows of tents, striding along through shadow and light, squinting into the dark slots between the tents. Nothing on the west side. He tried the east, the merry-go-round music in his ears.

The rear window of a food truck slapped open,

and a bucket was emptied just in front of him. The window slapped shut. He muttered and brushed at his splashed pantslegs. He walked on—and saw movement between two booths, in a space scarcely wide enough for a man. Light from a pole glared down into his eyes. He shaded them with his hand. And saw a thick-set man, back turned, crouching in the dark. Bohannon opened his mouth to call out and then said nothing. The man held a rifle. Light from the midway beyond him slid along its barrel. Bohannon caught the noise of a round being jacked into the chamber, and he knew the gun was his Winchester.

Bohannon eased himself between the canvas walls and smelled the bear smell. He tried to make no sound, stepping with care in case there were objects to fall over. He kept his eyes on the man, until the man lifted the gun to his shoulder to aim it. Then Bohannon looked for the target. Across the bright midway, Williams stood, holding a burrito that leaked chili sauce onto its paper wrapper. He was talking to a slight man with a neatly trimmed gray beard, who looked out of place at a carnival. *Distinguished* would be the easy word for him. His attitude seemed urgent.

"Hold it, Pancho," Bohannon said. "Don't shoot."

Pancho glanced over his shoulder, panic in his eyes, then turned back and fired the rifle. Bohannon lunged at him and got him in a choke hold. But Pancho dug a thick elbow into Bohannon's bound arm, and pain shot through Bohannon's shoulder, and he fell back. Pancho scrambled over him, a boot scraping Bohannon's cheekbone, another boot kicking off from Bohannon's stomach.

Gasping, sick, Bohannon staggered to his feet and lurched toward the rear of the slot. Light glared in his eyes again. He couldn't see Pancho. And this time he didn't hear him running off. A motorcycle engine spluttered to life. Its lights flicked on. Bohannon ran for it. But it jumped away, jouncing out of the light across the meadow, toward the dark highway.

See him ride a motorcycle. Not tonight.

There was turmoil around the burrito truck. The fat, brown, woman who ran it wailed loudly in Spanish. A skinny, blond youngster in a white coat hung over the counter like a broken marionette. His starchy little white cap lay trampled in the grass, and his blood dripped on it. Ambulance attendants climbed into the truck and got the boy out and onto a gurney, a blanket over him, plasma leaking into his arm from a plastic pouch. He was pale but breathing. Bohannon prayed the bullet had done him no mortal harm. The gurney slid with a clatter into the ambulance, the doors slammed, and together Bohannon and Gerard, in tan Sheriff's uniform, watched the ambulance rock slowly off down the midway, its siren moaning softly to warn people out of its track.

"He was aiming," Bohannon said, "at a man named Williams." He described Williams to Gerard. "He should be easy to find."

"What's the connection?" Gerard said.

"I don't know. The girl who looks after the animals"—Bohannon pointed at the big tent—"you might ask her. She said Pancho was scared of Williams. Maybe she knows why."

"He stole your rifle last night," Gerard said. He

was studying the way Bohannon's left arm was strapped across his chest, the way Bohannon's sleeve hung empty. "Did he shoot you with it first?"

"Used it for a club," Bohannon said. "If he'd shot, he would have hit somebody else, wouldn't he?"

"He's no marksman," Gerard admitted. "Why would he come clear up there to steal a rifle? Are you leveling with me?"

"It's what happened," Bohannon said. "He brought his van with the bear in it. Panicked my horses. He climbed the pole and cut off the electricity. Why? Ask him. That's not much of a motorcycle. He shouldn't be hard to catch up to."

From the big tent came the noise of a small band, bass drum, cymbals, sousaphone, a trumpet, a trombone, a piccolo. They were making a try at "The Entrance of the Gladiators," but it didn't sound as if they were going to finish together. Bohannon would have liked to see the show. Particularly the red-haired girl, whatever she did. But he was too tired. He said to Gerard:

"Can I go home now?"

"You should have reported the rifle stolen," Gerard said.

"Yeah, yeah," Bohannon said, and limped away.

It was another clear, dry morning. Everyone was at the pine table in the kitchen eating breakfast— the girl too. The sound of a car coming into the yard made her stand up and start hopping for the hall doorway. She had her plate in her hand and the fork on it rattled at every hop. Aching all over, Bohannon went to the kitchen door and looked out.

The car was a Sheriff's department vehicle and Gerard was already out of it and striding along the porch, the Winchester in his hands. When he saw Bohannon holding the screendoor open, he lifted the rifle and asked, "This yours?"

"Yes. Come in." Bohannon stood aside. Gerard entered the kitchen and stopped, looking at the girl with her plate in one hand and the other arm in a sling. "My niece," Bohannon said. "Lieutenant Gerard." He let the screendoor close.

Gerard nodded to the girl. "Like a hospital around here."

"She fell off a horse," Bohannon said. "Breakfast?"

"Coffee, if you can spare it." Gerard pulled out a chair at the table and sat down. He said to Stubbs and Rivera, "Gentlemen." He said to Bohannon, who brought the blue pot from the stove, "He wasn't hard to catch, because he stopped."

Bohannon poured coffee, and glanced at the girl. He wanted her out of the room, and he jerked his head. The problem was she couldn't open the door with the plate in her hand. He set the pot down, opened the door for her, shut it after her, came back to the table. He asked Gerard, "What did he tell you?"

"Nothing. He's dead. Left the motorcycle on the road shoulder and jumped off a two hundred foot cliff. Maybe he meant to hit the ocean. He hit the rocks. You know the place. Bull sea lions loaf around down there, bellowing. There's a good echo." Gerard dug in a starchy shirt pocket and brought out a note. "Stuck under the motorcycle brake lever." Bohannon took it. It.was in Spanish, and it said that Pancho was sorry to have killed the young man in the food truck. He asked forgiveness. Bohannon knew how he felt.

"The boy he shot," Bohannon said. "He's not dead?"

"He'll be fine." Gerard took back the note and laid photographs out on the table, color snapshots of a plumpish young woman and four young children, washed, combed, and in their Sunday best. "These were in Pancho's wallet." He turned one of them over. "See that rubber stamp?" Bohannon saw it—the name of a camera shop in Havana. Gerard said, "He had a Mexican passport and a green card, but he'd bought them someplace, fakes. The CIA has his fingerprints. He's a Cuban, not a refugee, a Castro man, in this country illegally." Gerard gathered up the snapshots. "Maybe Williams knew that, and was blackmailing him or something."

"Can't you find Williams?" Stubbs said.

"He never lights for long." Gerard pushed the note and snapshots into his shirt pocket. "He's stayed at three different motels in the area in the past three days. Only once was he Williams. He was Johnson first, then Freeman. When he rented that compact, he was Barnes. No such address."

Rivera said, "What will happen to the poor bear?"

"The San Francisco zoo is sending a man and a truck," Gerard said. "Meantime, he's a prisoner in cell eighteen."

Gerard drank his coffee and left. Rivera went to muck out stalls, Stubbs to coach a pair of young girls in low jumps inside the white rail paddock. Bohannon cleared the table, set the soiled dishes in the sink, went along the hall to collect the girl's plate. It lay on the chest of drawers. She herself sat in a stiff rocker and reproached him with her eyes. "You weren't going to notify the Sheriff."

"It wasn't about you," he said, "it was about my rifle. The man who came after you stole it. I went to get it back. There's a carnival in town. He worked for the carnival." Bohannon picked up her plate. "He had a trained bear act. Did you ever see it? The Tango Bear?"

She shook her head. She seemed honestly puzzled.

"He tried to kill somebody with my rifle." Bohannon gazed out the window down the canyon. "A man who calls himself Williams. Badly crippled up. Walks with aluminum crutches." Bohannon looked at the girl. "Him I think you do know."

She shook her head again, but too quickly this time, and fear showed in her eyes.

"He scares you senseless, he got me beaten up, and got a college boy shot at the carnival."

"I never wanted that," she said sharply.

"Then put a stop to it," Bohannon said. "Tell me what it's all about. Worse can happen. It already has. Tell me."

"I can't." It was a desperate cry, and tears ran down her scratched face. "You're lovely and kind and caring, and I want to tell you, because I know you'd understand. But I can't." She wiped at her tears with thin fingers. Her laugh was despairing. "That sounds stupid, doesn't it?"

"The Tango Bear man is dead," Bohannon said gravely. "When he couldn't get you out of here, when he couldn't kill the man on crutches, he killed himself. He had four small children and a wife back in Cuba. He's dead. Now, let me put it to you—whose fault is that?"

She reddened. "That's a terrible thing to say."

"It's a terrible thing to happen," he said.

"It isn't my fault." She jumped up. "Look—lend me money. Drive me to Fresno, the airport. I'll go. You won't have to worry about me anymore."

"I'll worry about you anyplace but right here."

"They wouldn't find me," she said. "They'd give up."

"Pancho didn't kill himself because Mr. Crutches is somebody who gives up." Bohannon opened the door. "You stay here till I can stop him, okay?" He turned back. "A slim, distinguished-looking man with a neat gray beard. Does he mean anything to you?"

She turned away, shaking her head. "Please. You have to stop asking me questions. No—I don't know him."

"You're a liar," Bohannon said, and left the room, and shut the door behind him.

Sorenson knew him. Sorenson showed up in a bright red fire patrol car at noon. He and Bohannon had been young deputy sheriffs together. When he came into the kitchen, he found Bohannon at the table, working on accounts payable with an electronic calculator. A very old portable typewriter was at Bohannon's elbow, for writing checks and, later in the day, granted the luck, tapping out bills. At the other side of the table, Stubbs used a

Blackwing pencil on a Strathmore drawing tablet. He would make a few lines, lift the pencil, look at Bohannon.

"Pale eyes," Bohannon muttered, scowling over the little white keys of the machine. "Blue or hazel. Pale, anyway."

Stubbs drew for a minute and held up the pad. "This him?"

Bohannon said, "What?" impatiently, then looked up and eyed the drawing critically. "More hair. He's got a good head of hair for a man his age—for a man of any age. That's about it, except for the hair."

Sorenson rattled the aluminum screen door. And Bohannon noticed him at last. Stubbs turned around on his chair. Sorenson had a long, horsey face and an aw-shucks smile. "It's hot out there. Thought you might spare me a beer. Been driving around trying to get people to cut back their brush. No rain in sight yet. Getting drier every day."

"Help yourself," Bohannon said, and bent over his bills again. Stubbs's pencil whispered on the rough paper. Sorenson opened the refrigerator, found a brown bottle, closed the refrigerator and, twisting the top off the bottle, ambled to the table, a gangly man. He peered over Stubbs's shoulder. "Hey, that's very good," he said, and rattled chair legs on the planks, and sat down. "What's it for?"

"Rivera's going to take it down to the carnival," Stubbs said, "and see if anybody there can identify him."

Sorenson's eyebrows went up. "You mean you drew that without even knowing who he is?"

"From Hack's description." Stubbs held the pad up to study it. "Never tried it before. Came out all right."

"It's a work of art." Sorenson tilted up the bottle and drank half its contents. He set the bottle down with a sigh. "Ah, that hits the spot." He took the pad from Stubbs and admired the drawing. "You going to give it to him?"

"If he wants it." Stubbs shrugged. "If we can find him."

Sorenson gave back the pad. "Try Solar Research Labs."

Bohannon stopped shuffling papers. "Up on the ridge?"

"He works there." Sorenson swallowed beer again, wiped his mouth with the back of his hand. "Dr. Farquar. I meet him on the road pretty often. Drives a big new Mercedes. Hard to miss. Always smiles and waves. Nice fellow."

"We'll see," Bohannon said.

It was the far ridge, the one that separated the cool of the coast from the heat of the inland valley. The buildings were plain white, big tilted saucers and dark, sundrinking slabs mounted on the roofs. Chainlink fence surrounded the place, topped by curls of razor wire. A severe signboard read SOLAR RESEARCH INSTITUTE, and in smaller letters gave information about whatever government agency in Washington, D. C. had charge of it. Uniformed soldiers stood outside the gates with guns, and inside the gates with guns. Signs fastened to the gates said ADMITTANCE RESTRICTED—U.S. GOVERNMENT INSTALLA-

TION. Bohannon stopped the pickup at a white plywood kiosk by the gates. It was a day for meeting old friends. Ruhrig looked out at him, a retired deputy.

"Hack," he said. "You got permission to go inside?"

"I didn't know I needed it," Bohannon said.

Ruhrig took off his security guard cap, and wiped sweat off his bald dome with a puffy hand. He smiled sadly. "You gotta have clearance, Hack. This here is a top secret outfit. You gotta fill out forms. They gotta be cleared with the Defense Department." He peered with bleary blue eyes. "You ever kiss a girl? Ever pee outdoors? No way a man of your depraved character will ever get in here."

"I just want to see Dr. Farquar," Bohannon said. "Don't they allow visitors?"

"You want to visit," Ruhrig said, "guess they figure you can visit after work hours."

"Do you know Farquar?" Bohannon said. "When does he get off work? I'll wait out here."

"He didn't come in today. Yesterday, either."

Bohannon dug out his wallet, and from it took a business card. "Can you get this to his secretary or somebody? I want him to call me." He reached out the pickup window. "Let me have a pen." Ruhrig found a pen on an untidy shelf inside the kiosk, and handed it to Bohannon. Bohannon wrote *Urgent!* on the back of the card. He passed card and pen to Ruhrig. "If he shows up or telephones in to his office, maybe they'll put him in touch with me."

"I'll send it inside," Ruhrig said. He read what Bohannon had written. "What's it about?"

"I wish I knew," Bohannon said. "Maybe he'll tell me."

A shadow fell across Ludlow's apple orchards, taking the shine from the leaves and the young fruit. Bohannon frowned up through the dusty windshield. Sure enough. Wind was moving clouds in from the ocean. He gave a little smile. With luck, the dry spell was about to end. Sorenson could stop worrying about people cutting back their dry brush, and Bohannon could stop worrying about his horses. Taking the long loop of rising trail around the little valley, he watched the cloud shadows cross sloping grassland, where stocky whiteface cattle browsed.

The road began a steeper climb. He shifted gears. The mossy oaks and shadowy creek of the canyon bottom dropped away, the apple orchard, the grazing cattle, the coolness. He was in rock and dry brush country now, and the sun glared hot through the windshield. The windshield spiderwebbed. A bullet plunked into the seatback beside him. He ducked. It was a no-good reflex. His foot searched for the brake pedal. Another no-good reflex. He didn't want to stop. If you were going to be a target, be a moving target. He crouched over the wheel, gripping it with the only good hand he had, and he throttled the old pickup hard, weaving from side to side of the narrow road.

This time he heard the slap of the gun. So the bullet had missed him. The next bullet spanged off the metal of the truck bed before he heard the gunshot. The road made a sharp angle. He braked for a second, then hit the throttle hard. Roadside dust swirled up. The right rear wheel almost went over. Then the road topped out. He could see well from here. He risked slowing for a minute to take a look. At first the world looked empty of anyone but him. Then sunlight winked off glass. He dimly heard the slam of a car door. He located it, among scrub oak on a rise—the beige compact. The noise of its four little cylinders starting reached him on the quiet air. The car lurched down toward the road.

Bohannon jumped out of the pickup, lifted the seat, dug a hammer from among rusty tools there, and knocked a hole in the crackled windshield glass so he could see to drive. He put hammer and seat back, scrambled into the cab, kicked off the floor what loose glass he could, and slammed the door. He let go the handbrake and drove on. He knew these canyons, every twist and tack. He would soon lose Williams.

To sneak home by crooked back trails would waste time, but he would arrive breathing. The girl had made breathing important to him again. She needed him. He had just begun to grasp why. And how much. The clouds blocked out the sun, now. Their whiteness began to smudge. The wind took on a cold, damp edge. He hoped a storm was the worst that was going to happen tonight. But he didn't believe it.

It was bad enough. By four-thirty rain fell heavily. It brought night early to Rodd canyon. Stubbs herded the last of the horses down from the pasture in near dark. A rubber poncho had kept the old man from getting too wet, but nothing had done that for the horses. It was an hour before Stubbs and Rivera had dried them off and closed the doors on the last of the box stalls, and come into the kitchen where the girl sat and watched Bohannon cook. He had told her about Williams shooting out his windshield.

"If you get rid of me, he'll stop," she said. "Take me where I can get a plane."

"They won't be flying tonight," Bohannon said.

Thunder crashed, lightning flared, the wind rose and grew hoarse, shaking the ranch house. In the middle of supper the lights went out. After supper, Bohannon took the girl to her room with a kerosene lamp. He locked the window, drew the curtains, and left her with Rivera, the rifle, and chess pieces set out on a little table between them. Stubbs hurried back to the stables.

Bohannon washed the dishes by lamplight, set out files and forms on the table, and began to type statements, leaning close to the old portable to read what he typed. It was nearly eight by his watch when the screendoor hinges creaked and knuckles rapped the wooden door. Bohannon went and pulled it open. Farquar stood there in a pale fly-front raincoat, rain-darkened on the shoulders. Rain dripped from the brim of his waterproof hat and from his neat gray beard.

"You wanted to see me?" he said.

"Come in," Bohannon said. Cold wet air blew in with the man. The doorway lit up with a lightning flash. Bohannon closed the door. Thunder split the sky overhead. Bohannon said, "Let me take your coat. Sit down."

Farquar shook his head, read his watch. "I'll stand, thank you. I'm running late. What is this about?"

"A man with crippled legs who calls himself Williams." Bohannon got the Old Crow from a shadowy cupboard, and brought the bottle and two glasses to the table. "He tried to kill me today. I thought you could explain why."

Farquar looked around at the gently lamplit room. "What would make you think that?"

"You were talking to Williams last night at the carnival. By the burrito truck. When there was a shooting, you and Williams vanished. Together. Who is he, Dr. Farquar?"

"I'm afraid you've mistaken me for someone else."

"If that were so," Bohannon said, "you wouldn't be here. Sit down. Have a drink. It's a good night for it. Why did Williams come here the other morning to scout my place? Why did he send someone to break in here that night? Why did that same messenger then try to kill Williams at the carnival, and having failed to do that"—Bohannon poured whiskey—"kill himself? I'm talking about Pancho, the bear trainer."

Farquar was silent. Bohannon looked at him. Farquar's paleness and startlement were plain even in the poor light. He took hold of a chair back, as if to steady himself. He said faintly, hoarsely, "Dear God. You've got her. Here." He looked over his shoulder, and he was afraid. He stepped around the table and the hand trembled that he laid on Bohannon's shoulder. "Where is she? Bring her to me at once."

"Not 'How is she?'" Bohannon handed him a

glass. "She broke an arm and sprained an ankle jumping out of your car over yonder the other night. Wonder is she wasn't killed." Dumbly Farquar accepted the glass. Bohannon raised his. "Here's to fatherly concern. She is your daughter, right? She's got your eyes. Down to the fear in them."

"You're wasting time." Farquar set his glass down and headed for the inner door. "Jennifer? Where are you?" He opened the door and shouted along the hall. "It's Daddy. Please be reasonable, now. You must come with me."

"Where?" Bohannon stood behind him.

"To Europe. I've been appointed to a fine position there." He pulled airline tickets from a pocket and waved them helplessly. "She doesn't want to go."

"Emphatically," Bohannon said, and saw light fall into the hall from her room. She came out, stood for a moment staring, then hobbled slowly toward her father. "I won't," she said. "You know I won't."

Farquar said, "But Williams will kill you."

"Why would he do that?" Bohannon said.

"It could all have been so simple." Farquar sounded ready to weep. "Why wouldn't you just come quietly? Now it's turned to a matter of life and death."

"It was always that." She put her arms around him, kissed his cheek, pushed away from him. "You go. You'll be all right. You'll have what you wanted."

"But there's no reason why you—" he began. And stopped with a small cry. Williams came out the door from the girl's room. He had the Winchester clutched under his arm. "Young ladies Jennifer's age," he said, in a country-western twang, "don't always take to what's reasonable."

"That's no excuse to murder them," Farquar cried.

"He doesn't need excuses," Bohannon said. "It's his way of life. What's it about, Mr. Johnson-Freeman-Williams-Barnes? If you think she's given away your secret, you're mistaken. She hasn't said one word."

Short legs scuffling on the boards, big shoulders heaving, Williams came on with a grin and a chuckle. "You just didn't ask the right questions. There's folks who know how." He jerked the rifle barrel at them. "Get in the kitchen, please? Where we can all be comfortable?" The thunder cracked again, echoing down the canyon. Williams told Bohannon's back, "You serve up some weather, here."

"It's my father's secret," Jennifer said. "I won't betray my father. Even though I think he's wrong. But you can't understand that, can you? You can go your way in peace, Mr. Williams. So can he."

"I like to be very sure," Williams said. "Sit down." She sat. He stood. "Dr. Farquar, you are not going to be on flight 709 to Berlin if you don't start pretty soon. San Francisco's quite a drive in the rain."

"Let me take her," Farquar begged.

"Get a move on, doctor," Williams said softly.

"No. Not without Jennifer." Farquar dug frantically in his coat. "I won't leave her here to die." A little black revolver was in his hand. He caught the girl's wrist and brought her up off her chair. He backed toward the kitchen door, she hobbling beside him, eyes wide with fear in the lamplight. She looked terribly young. Williams fumbled with the rifle. Bohannon blew out the lamp.

The rifle blazed. Its explosion was deafening. Bohannon dropped to the floor. The kitchen door opened. A gust of wet wind blew across the floor. Lightning flashed, and by its glare Bohannon located Williams, who was struggling to cock the gun again. "Run like hell," Bohannon shouted, lunged low at Williams, and knocked his crutches from under him. The man fell. The rifle clattered. Bohannon groped for it, found it, tottered to his feet. Williams got a grip on Bohannon's ankle. The man was strong. Bohannon used the rifle the only way he could with one bad arm, the way Pancho had used it on him—as a club.

He wheeled a rented car into the yard at sundown two days later, switched off its engine, and sat looking at the place, the long, low-roofed white stables, the fences, the trees, the browsing horses in the meadows newly greened by the rain. He was grateful to be back. He got stiffly out of the car and breathed the fresh air deeply. The smell of law-enforcement buildings was about all he'd breathed for forty-eight hours. From San Luis to Sacramento, where the CIA had offices. He knocked heels along the porch and opened the kitchen screendoor. Stubbs was at the stove.

"Not turkey hash again," Bohannon said.

"You hurt my feelings," Stubbs said. "It's beef stew."

Rivera rose from the table to fetch a plate and eating utensils for Bohannon. The boy looked pale.

His head was bandaged. When he had risen to follow the girl out of the room after she'd heard her father's voice, Williams had hit him from behind. "I am ashamed," he said.

"Forget it." Bohannon sat down. "Bring me a glass with ice and the whiskey, all right? And I'll tell you all about it. I don't want any questions. I've done nothing but answer questions ever since I left." He sighed, lit a cigarette, and took the glass and bottle Rivera brought. "And I'll have to answer them all over again down the line when there's a trial." He poured himself a drink.

"Who's Williams?" Stubbs said. "A Roosky spy?"

"Don't do that," Bohannon said. "Just listen. Williams works for Williams. Near as I can gather, anyplace and everyplace in the world. He's a broker. He buys and sells."

"Secrets? Did Farquar pass him some kind of new weapon they been working on up at that solar research place?"

"There you go again," Bohannon said. "Yes, but not for cash. For an ideal. To save humanity. He figured if both sides had this new horror, there'd be a standoff. Williams arranged for that post in East Germany. Farquar had quietly settled his affairs here. He was just going to disappear."

Stubbs took large bowls out of a cupboard. "Only his daughter found out. That how it went?"

"And confronted him, tried to persuade him to turn Williams in. Farquar might be excused, then. He wouldn't listen. And now he said she had to leave with him. When she jumped and ran instead, he panicked and told Williams."

Stubbs ladled the bowls full of stew. "And Williams decided she had to be killed to keep her quiet. Couldn't manage it himself, so he sent the bear man. Why him?"

"Williams has a list of vulnerable people. Pancho was handy. Williams threatened his family back in Cuba."

Stubbs limped to the table and set down steaming bowls. "How's the girl? How did she take it?"

Bohannon had happened on her this morning in a courthouse corridor. She looked forlorn. He said, "Don't feel bad. You did what you thought was right. You did your best."

"It wasn't good enough," she said bleakly.

"It almost never is," Bohannon said.

Surf

Lieutenant Ken Barker of the LAPD shared a gray-green office with too many other men, too many gray-green metal desks and file cabinets, too many phones that kept crying for attention like new life in a sad maternity ward. He had a broken nose. Under his eyes were bruises. He wore beard stubble. His teeth were smoky. He scowled across a sprawl of papers and spent styrofoam cups. He said:

"Yes, Robinson was murdered. On the deck of his apartment. In that slum by the sea called Surf. Shot clean through the head. He went over the rail, was dead when he hit the sand. There's nothing wrong with the case. The DA is happy. What do you want to mess it up for?"

"I don't." Dave shed a wet trenchcoat, hung it over a chairback, sat on another chair. "I just want to know why Robinson made Bruce K. Shevel the beneficiary of his life insurance policy. Didn't he have a wife, a mother, a girlfriend?"

"He had a boyfriend, and the boyfriend killed him. Edward Earl Lily, by name. With a deer rifle, a thirty-thirty. Probably Robinson's. He owned one." Barker blinked. "It's weird, Dave. I mean, what have you got—an instinct for this kind of case?"

"Coincidence," Dave said. "What does probably mean—Robinson was 'probably' killed with his own gun."

Barker found a bent cigarette. "Haven't located it."

"Where does Lily say it is?"

"Claims he never saw it." Barker shuffled papers, hunting a match. "But it'll be in the surf someplace along there. Or buried in the sand. We're raking for it." Dave leaned forward and snapped a thin steel gas lighter. Barker said thanks and asked through smoke, "You don't like it? Why not? What's wrong with it?"

Dave put the lighter away. "Ten years ago, Bruce K. Shevel jacked up his car on one of those trails in Topanga Canyon to change a tire, and the car rolled over on him and cost him the use of his legs. He was insured with us. We paid. We still pay. Total disability. I'd forgotten him. But I remembered him today when I checked Robinson's policy. Shevel looked to me like someone who'd tried self-mutilation to collect on his accident policy."

"Happens, doesn't it?" Barker said.

"People won't do anything for money." Dave's smile was thin. "But they will hack off a foot or a hand for it. I sized Shevel up for one of those. His business was in trouble. The policy was a fat one. I don't think paralysis was in his plans. But it paid better. The son of a bitch grinned at me from that hospital bed. He knew I knew and there was no way to prove it."

"And there still isn't," Barker said. "Otherwise you could stop paying and put him in the slams. And it pisses you off that he took you. And now you see a chance to get him." Barker looked into one of the empty plastic cups, made a face, stood up. "You'd like him to have killed Robinson."

He edged between desks to a coffee urn at the window end of the room, the glass wall end. Dave followed. Through vertical metal sun slats outside, gray rain showed itself like movie grief. "I'd like Robinson to have died peacefully in bed of advanced old age." Dave pulled a cup from a chrome tube bolted to a window strut and held the cup while Barker filled it. "And since he didn't, I'd sure as hell like him to have left his money to someone else."

"We interviewed Shevel." Next to the hot plate that held the coffee urn was cream substitute in a widemouth brown bottle and sugar in little cellophane packets. Barker used a yellow plastic spoon to stir some of each into his coffee. "We interviewed everybody in Robinson's little black book." He led the way back to his desk, sat down, twisted out his cigarette in a big glass ashtray glutted with butts. "And Shevel is a wheelchair case."

Dave tasted his coffee. Weak and tepid. "A wheelchair case can shoot a gun."

Barker snorted. "Have you seen where Robinson lived?"

"I'll go look. But first tell me about Lily." Dave sat down, then eyed the desk. "Or do I need to take your time? Shall I just read the file?"

"My time? I'd only waste it sleeping. And I'm out of practice. I wouldn't do it well." Barker glanced sourly at the folders, forms, photographs on his desk, then hung another cigarette from his mouth and leaned forward so Dave could light it. "Lily is a trick Robinson picked up at the Billy Budd. You know the place?"

Dave nodded. "Ocean Front Walk."

"Robinson tended bar there. The kid's a hustler but way out of Robinson's league. A hundred bucks a night and/or a part in your next TV segment, sir. But somehow Robinson managed to keep him. Eight, ten weeks, anyway—" The phone on Barker's desk jangled. He lifted the receiver, listened, grunted, cradled the receiver. "—Till he was dead. Lily ran, but not far and not clever. He was better at crying. You know the type. Muscles, but a real girl. Kept sobbing that he loved Robinson and why would he kill him?"

"And why would he?" Dave lit a cigarette.

Barker shrugged. "Probably hysteria. Toward the end they were fighting a lot. About money. Robinson had bought him fancy clothes, an Omega watch, a custom surf board. They'd been pricing Porsches and Aston-Martins on the lots. But Robinson was broke. He'd hocked his stereo, camera, projector. He was borrowing from friends."

"What friends?" Dave asked. "Shevel?"

"Among others," Barker said. "Which kind-of louses up your theory, doesn't it? Shevel didn't need to shoot anybody for their insurance money. He's loaded."

The boy who opened the door had dressed fast. He still hadn't buttoned his white coverall with *L A Marina* stitched on the pocket. Under the coverall his jockeys were on inside out and backward. Below the nick of navel in his flat brown belly a label read *Pilgrim*. He was chicano and wore his hair long. He looked confused. "He thought it would be the layouts."

"It isn't," Dave said. "Brandstetter is my name. Death claims investigator, Medallion Life. I'm looking for Bruce K. Shevel. Is he here?"

"Brand—what?" the boy said.

At his back a dense jungle of philodendrons climbed a trellis to the ceiling. From beyond it a voice said, "Wait a minute, Manuel." A pair of chrome spoked wheels glittered into view, a pair of wasted legs under a lap robe, a pair of no color eyes that had never forgiven anyone anything. "I remember you. What do you want?"

"Arthur Thomas Robinson is dead," Dave said.

"I've already told the police what I know."

"Not all of it." Wind blew cold rain across the back of Dave's neck. He turned up the trench coat collar. "You left out the part that interests me— that you're the beneficiary of his life insurance."

Shevel stared. There was no way for his face to grow any paler. It was parchment. But his jaw dropped. When he shut it, his dentures clicked. "You must be joking. There's got to be some mistake."

"There's not." Dave glanced at the rain. "Can I come in and talk about it?"

Shevel's mouth twitched. "Did you bring the check?"

Dave shook his head. "Murder has a way of slowing down the routine."

"Then there's nothing to talk about." The wheelchair was motorized. It started to turn away.

"Why would he name you?" Dave asked.

Shrug. "We were old friends."

Dave studied the Chicano boy who was watching them with something frantic in his eyes. "Friends?"

"Oh, come in, come in," Shevel snarled, and wheeled out of sight. Dave stepped onto deep beige carpeting and the door closed behind him. But when he turned to hand the trenchcoat over, there was no one to take it. Manuel had buttoned up and left. Dave laid the coat over his arm and went around the leafy screen. A long, handsome room stretched to sliding glass doors at its far end that looked down on a marina where little white boats waited row on row like children's coffins in the rain. Shevel rattled ice and glasses at a low bar. "I met Robbie in the hospital," he said, "ten years ago." He came wheeling at Dave, holding out a squat studded glass in which dark whiskey islanded an ice cube. "Just as I met you." His smile was crooked. "He worked there. An orderly."

"And you brought him along to look after you when the hospital let you go." Dave took the drink. "Thanks."

"Robbie had good hands." Shevel aimed the chair at the planter. From under it somewhere he took a small green plastic watering can. He tilted it carefully into the mulch under the climbing vines. "And patience."

"Who took his place?"

"No one. No one could. This apartment is arranged so that I don't need day to day help." Shevel set the watering can back. "The market sends in food and liquor." He drank from his glass. "I can cook my own meals. I'm able to bathe myself and so on. A cleaning woman comes in twice a week. I have a masseur on call."

"Manuel?" Dave wondered.

"Not Manuel," Shevel said shortly and drank again.

"You publish a lot of magazines," Dave said. "How do you get to your office? Specially equipped car?"

"No car," Shevel said. "Cars are the enemy." He purred past Dave and touched a wall switch. A panel slid back. Beyond gleamed white wet-look furniture, a highgloss white desk stacked with papers, a white electric typewriter, a photocopy machine. Blowup color photos of naked girls muraled the walls. "I don't go to the office. My work comes to me. And there's the telephone." He swallowed more whiskey. "You remember the telephone?" He touched the switch and the panel slid closed.

Dave asked, "When did Robinson quit you?"

"Eight months, two weeks and six days ago," Shevel said. He said it grimly with a kind of inverse satisfaction, like counting notches in a gun butt.

"Did he give a reason?"

"Reason?" Shevel snorted and worked on his drink again. "He felt old age creeping up on him. He was all of thirty-two. He decided he wanted to be the one who was looked after, for a change."

"No quarrels? No hard feelings?"

"Just boredom." Shevel looked at his glass but it was empty. Except for the ice cube. It still looked new. He wheeled abruptly back to the bar and worked the bottle again. Watching him, Dave tried his drink for the first time. Shevel bought good Bourbon with Medallion's money. Shevel asked, "If there'd been hard feelings, would he have come back to borrow money?"

"That might depend on how much he needed it," Dave said. "Or thought he did. I hear he was desperate."

Shevel's eyes narrowed. "What does that mean?"

"Trying to keep a champagne boy on a beer income."

"Exactly." Shevel's mouth tightened like a drawstring purse. "He never had any common sense."

"So you didn't lend him anything," Dave said.

"I told him not to be a fool. Fortynine percent of the world's population is male." Shevel's chair buzzed. He steered it back, stopped it, tilted his glass, swallowed half the new drink. He looked toward the windows where the rain was gray. His voice was suddenly bleak. "I'm sorry he's dead. He was life to me for a long time."

"I'll go." Dave walked to the bar, set down his glass, began shrugging into the trenchcoat. "Just two more questions. Manuel. Does he take you deer hunting?"

Shevel looked blank.

Dave said, "Your thirty-thirty. When did you use it last?"

Shevel squinted. "What are you talking about?"

"A deer rifle. Winchester. Remington."

"Sorry." His bony fingers teased his white wig. He simpered like a skid row barroom floozy. "I've always preferred indoor sports." He was suddenly drunk. He looked Dave up and down hungrily. "Next question."

"Those magazines of yours," Dave said. "The new

Supreme Court decision on obscenity. You're going to have to do some retooling—right?"

Shevel's eyes got their old hardness back. "It's been on the drawingboards for months. A whole new line. Home crafts. Dune buggies. Crossword puzzles. And if you're suggesting I shot Robbie with his rifle in order to get the money to finance the change-over, then you don't know much about publishing costs. Ten thousand dollars wouldn't buy the staples."

"But you do know how much the policy paid."

The crooked smile came back. "Naturally. I bought it for him. Years ago." The smile went away. "How typical of him to have forgotten to take my name off it."

"And the thirty-thirty. Did you buy that too?"

"I paid for it, of course. He had no money."

"I'll just bet he didn't," Dave said.

The development may have looked sharp to start with but it had gone shabby fast. It was on the coast road at the north end of Surf, which had gone shabby a long time ago. You couldn't see the development from the coast road. You had to park between angled white lines on the tarmacked shoulder and walk to a cliff where an iron pipe railing was slipping, its cement footings too near the crumbling edge.

Below, along a narrow rock and sand curve of shore stood apartment buildings. The tinwork vents on the roofs were rusting. Varnish peeled from rafter ends and wooden decks. The stucco had been laid on thin. It was webbed with cracks. Chunks had broken out at corners showing tarpaper and chickenwire underneath.

Dave saw what Ken Barker had meant. The only access to the place was down cement steps, three long flights against the cliff face. There'd been too much sand in the cement. Edges had crumbled. Today rain washed dirt and pebbles across the treads and made them treacherous. No—no wheelchair case could get down there. He was about to turn back when, the way it will sometimes for a second, the surf stopped booming. It charged and fell heavily today, like a big, tired army under one of those generals that never gives up. But it breathed.

And in the sudden silence he heard from below a voice, raised in argument, protest, complaint. He went on down. The iron rail was scabby with corrosion. His hand came away rusty. He left cement for a boardwalk over parts of which sand had drifted, sand now dark and sodden with rain. He passed the backs of buildings, slope-top metal trash modules, the half open doors of laundry rooms. The voice kept on. He turned between two buildings to walk for the beach front.

The voice came from halfway up wooden steps to a second story deck. A small man stood there under a clear plastic umbrella. He was arguing up at the legs of a young black police officer above him on the second story deck. The officer wore a clear plastic slicker.

The little man shouted, "But I'm the God damn owner of the God damn place. A taxpayer. It's not Chief Gates that pays you—it's me. You know what the taxes are here? No—well, I'm not going to tell you because I hate to see a strong man cry. But they got to be paid, friend, if I rent it or don't rent it. And have you looked at it? I was screwed by the contractor. It's falling apart. Nineteen months old and falling apart. I'm suing the son of a bitch but the lawyers are breaking me. Not to mention the mortgage. A storm like this, carpets get soaked, plaster falls down. Could be happening in there right now. Why do you want to make things worse for me?"

Dave climbed the steps. When he'd come up to the little man, the officer said, "Mr. Brandstetter. That make three. This one. Robinson's ex-boss. Now you." His grin was very white. "This a real popular spot this morning."

"Turning people away, right?" Dave said. "Because the apartment's sealed, waiting for the DA?" He looked past the little man. Up the beach, a clutch of slickered cops was using a drag with deep teeth on the sand. Plastic wrapped their caps, their shoes. Nothing about them looked happy. It was work for tractors. But there was no way to get tractors down here.

The black officer said, "DA been and gone."

"Yeah." The little man goggled at Dave through big horn rims. "They talk about human rights. What happened to property rights? I own the place but I get treated like a thief. I can't get in till Robinson's brother comes and collects his stuff." His nose was red. And not from sunburn. There hadn't been any sun this month. "You're not his brother, are you?"

"Not the way you mean," Dave said. And to the officer, "Flag me when he comes, will you?" He went down the stairs and down the rain-runnelled beach. The sergeant he talked to wore plain clothes and no hat. His name was Slocum. Rain plastered strands of pale red hair to his freckled scalp. Dave said, "What about the surf?"

"Running too high. You can't work a launch on it. Not close in where we have to look. Keep washing you up all the time." He glanced bitterly at the muddy sky. "Storm doesn't quit, we'll never find it."

"The storm could be your friend," Dave said. "Ought to wash anything ashore—all that power." And fifty yards off a cop yelled in the rain, bent in the rain, picked something out of the muddy surf, came with it at a trot, waving it above his head, like a movie Apache who'd got the wrong room at Western Costume. "See?" Dave said.

"No wonder you're rich," Slocum said. It was a rifle. The cop offered it. Slocum shook his head. "You've got gloves, I don't. You hold it. Let me just look at it." He just looked at it while the cop turned it over and it dripped. "Thirty-thirty Remington," Slocum said. "Eight years old but like new. Won't act like new—not unless they get the seawater out of it right away."

"Sea water doesn't erase prints," Dave said and turned back toward the apartments because he heard his name called above the slam of surf, the hiss of rain. The black officer was waving an arm from the deck. A bulky man was with him. Dave jogged back. The landlord was yammering to a girl with ragged short hair in a Kobe coat at the foot of the stairs but there wasn't any hope in his voice now. Dave went up the stairs.

"Reverend Merwin Robinson," the black officer said. "Mr. Brandstetter. Insurance."

"Something wrong with the insurance?" The reverend had a hoarse voice. The kind you get from shouting—at baseball games or congregations. A thick man, red-faced. A big crooked vein bulged at one temple.

"What's wrong with it is the beneficiary," Dave said.

Robinson stiffened, glared. "I don't understand."

"Not you," Dave said. "Bruce K. Shevel."

Robinson blinked. "You must be mistaken."

"That's what Shevel said," Dave said.

"But I'm Arthur's only living relative. Neither of us has anyone else. And he'd left Shevel. Said he never wanted to see him again."

"He saw him again," Dave said. "Tried to borrow money from him. I gather he saw you too."

The minister's mouth twitched. "Never at my invitation. And years would go by. He knew my stand. On how he lived. The same saintly mother raised us. He knew what the Bible says about him and his kind."

"But lately he tried to borrow money," Dave said.

"He did." The black officer had opened the glass wall panel that was the apartment door. Robinson saw, grunted, went in. Dave followed. The room was white shag carpet, long low fake-fur couches, swag lamps in red and blue pebbled glass. "Of course I refused. My living comes from collection plates. For the glory of God and His beloved Son. Not to buy fast automobiles for descendents of the brothels of Sodom."

"I don't think they had descendents," Dave said. "Anyway, did you have that kind of money?"

"My church is seventy years old. We've had half a dozen fires from faulty wiring. The neighborhood the church serves is just as old and just as poor." Robinson glanced at a shiny kitchenette where a plaster Michaelangelo David stood on a counter with plastic ferns. He went on to an alcove at the room's end, opened and quickly closed again a door to a bathroom papered with color photos of naked men from *Playgirl*, and went into a room where the ceiling was squares of gold-veined mirror above a round, tufted bed.

Dave watched him open drawers, scoop out the contents, dump them on the bed. Not a lot of clothes. A few papers. He slid back closet doors. Little hung inside. He took down what there was, spilling coat hangers, clumsily stooped, pushed the papers into a pocket, then bundled all the clothes into his arms and turned to face Dave. "That ten thousand dollars would have meant a lot to my church—new wiring, shingles, paint, new flooring to replace what's rotted—" He broke off, a man used to having dreams cancelled. He came at the door with his bundle of dead man's clothes and Dave made way for him. "Well, at least these will keep a few needy souls warm for the winter." He lumbered off down the length of the apartment, on to the deck and out of sight.

Dave looked after him. The view was clear from this room to the deck—maybe forty feet. Lily could have stood here with the 30-30. At that distance the bullet hole wouldn't be too messy. Dave went for the door where cold, damp air came in. Also the little man who owned the place. He collided with Dave.

"Your turn," Dave said.

"It rents furnished," the little man said. "A

preacher, for God sake! Crookeder than a politician. Did you see? Did he take kitchen stuff? I saw that bundle. Anything could have been in it. All the kitchen stuff stays with the place. Sheets, towels? All that's mine." He rattled open kitchen drawers, cupboards, slammed them shut again, dodged into the bathroom, banged around in there—"Jesus, look what that fag did to the walls!"—shot out of the bathroom and into the bedroom. Merwin Robinson had left the chest drawers hanging. From the doorway Dave could see their total emptiness. The little man stopped in front of them. His shoulders sagged. In relief or disappointment?

"All okay?" Dave asked.

"What? Oh, yeah. Looks like it." He didn't sound convinced.

Downstairs Dave pressed a buzzer next to a glass panel like the one directly above that had opened into Arthur Thomas Robinson's apartment. While he'd talked to the dead man's brother and the black officer he'd looked past their wet shoes through the slats in the deck and seen the short-haired girl go into this apartment. She came toward him now with *Daily Variety* in her hand, looking as if she didn't want to be bothered. She still wore the Kobe coat but her hair wasn't short any more. She had on a blond wig out of an Arthur Rackham illustration—big and fuzzy. She slid the door. A smell of fresh coffee came out.

"Were you at home when Robinson was killed?"

She studied him. Without makeup she looked like

a ten year old boy dressed up as the dandelion fairy. "You a cop?"

He told her who he was, gave her a card. "The police like to think Lily killed him because it's easy, it will save the taxpayers money. I'm not so sure."

She tilted her head, "Whose money will that save?"

"Not Medallion's," he said. "I'd just like to see it go to somebody else."

"Than?" She shivered. "Look—come in." He did that and she slid the door to and put the weather outside where it belonged. "Coffee?" Dropping *Variety* on a couch like the ones upstairs, she led him to the kitchenette, talking. "Who did Robbie leave his money to?" She filled pottery mugs from a glass urn. "It's funny, thinking of him having money to leave when he was hitting on me and everybody else for twenty here, twenty there." She came around the counter, pushed a tall, flower-cushioned bar stool at Dave and perched on one herself. "He was really sick."

"Sick?" Dave tried the coffee. Rich and good.

"Over that Eddie. Nothing—beautiful junk. Like this pad. Robbie was nice, a really nice, gentle, sweet, warm human being. Of all things to happen to him!" She took a mouthful of coffee, froze with the cup halfway to the countertop, stared, swallowed. "You don't mean Robbie left Ed Lily that money?"

"That would be too easy," Dave said. "No—he left it to Bruce K. Shevel."

"You're kidding," she said.

Dave twitched an eyebrow, sighed, got out cigarettes. "That's what everybody thinks. Including

Shevel." He held the pack for her to take one, took one himself, lit both. He dropped the lighter into his pocket. "Was Shevel ever down here?"

"How? He was a wheelchair case. Robbie told me about him. It was one of the reasons he chose this place. So Shevel couldn't get to him. The stairs. Why would he leave Shevel his money?"

"An oversight, I expect. After all, what was he— thirty-two? At that age, glimmerings of mortality are still dim. Plenty of time to make changes. Or maybe because Shevel had bought him the policy, he thought he owed him something."

"Robbie owed him? That's a laugh. He used him like a slave for ten years. If anything, it was the other way around. Shevel owed him. But he wouldn't shell out a dime when Robbie asked for it."

"So I hear," Dave said. "Tell me about Lily."

She shrugged. "You know the type. Dime a dozen in this town. They drift in on their thumbs, all body, no brains. If they even get as far as a producer, they end up with their face in his pillow. Then it's back to Texas or Tennessee to pump gas for the rest of their lives. Only Eddie was just a little different. Show business he could live without. Hustling was surer and steadier. He always asked for parts in pictures but he settled for cash. A born whore. Loved it.

"I tried to tell Robbie. He wouldn't listen. Couldn't hear. Gone on the little shit, really gone. You want to know something? Eddie hadn't been here a week when he tried to get me into the sack." Her mouth twitched a half grin. "I told him, 'I don't go to bed with fags.' 'I'm not a fag,' was all he said.

As if I and every other woman in the place didn't know that. Woman. Man. Everybody—except Robbie." She turned her head to look down the room at the glass front wall, the gray rain beyond it, the deserted beach, the muddy slop of surf. "Poor Robbie! What happens to people?" She turned back for an answer.

"In his case," Dave said, "murder."

"Yeah." She rolled her cigarette morosely against a little black ashtray. "And he never said a wrong word to Eddie. Never. Eddie was all over him all the time—I want this, I want that. You promised to introduce me to so-and-so. Take me here, take me there."

Dave looked at the ceiling. "Soundproofing another thing they cheated the owner on?"

"I got pretty familiar with Robbie's record collection. Sure, I could hear damn near every word. And a lot that wasn't words. The bedroom's right over mine too."

"Was that where the shot came from?" Dave asked.

"I wasn't here. Didn't I tell you? I was on location in Montana. Up to my elbows in flour in a tumble-down ranch house with little kids tugging at my skirts and my hair hanging over one eye. Twenty seconds on film. All that way on Airwest for twenty seconds."

"Too bad," Dave said. "Were you ever up there?"

"Robbie's? Yeah, for drinks. Now and then."

"Ever see a rifle?"

"They found it, didn't they?" She jerked the big fuzzy wig toward the beach. "Talking to Dieterle, I saw the cop fish it out of the kelp and run to you with it. You brought them luck. They were raking for it all day yesterday too."

"But did you ever see it in the apartment?"

She shrugged. "It was probably in a closet." She drank some coffee and frowned. "Wait a minute. I helped Robbie move in. No, I didn't know him. I parked up at the cliff edge and there he was with all this stuff to carry. I just naturally offered to help. And I hung around helping him settle in and we had a drink."

"Easy to know," Dave said.

"A bartender," she said. "Had been since he was a kid, except for that period with Shevel. Easy friendliness is part of a bartender's stock in trade—right? Only he didn't fake it. He honestly liked people. Those old aunties Lauder and White fell all over themselves to get him back. Business has doubled since he took over. If he owned his own place he'd make a bundle." She remembered he was dead and sadness happened in her face. "Except for one thing."

Dave worked on his coffee. "Which was?"

"He also trusted people. And that's for losers."

"About the rifle?" he prompted her.

"He didn't own one," she said flatly. "I'd have seen it while we were putting away his stuff. No rifle. But I can tell you one thing. If there'd been one, Eddie could have used it. He used to talk about hunting rabbits when he was a kid back in Oklahoma."

"Thanks." Dave tilted up the mug, drained it, set it on the counter, got off the stool. "And for the coffee." He checked his watch. "But now it's out into the cold rain and the mean streets again."

"Aw," she said.

Climbing the gritty stairs up the cliff face, he still heard the surf. But as he neared the top there was the wet tire sibilance of traffic on the the coast road and the whine of a car engine that didn't want to start. At the railing, the little landlord, Dieterle, sat in a faded old Triumph, swearing. Dave walked over and wondered in a shout if he could help. Dieterle, with a sour twist of his mouth, gave up.

"Ah, it'll catch, it'll catch. Son of a bitch knows I'm in a hurry. Always acts like this." Rain had misted the big round lenses of his glasses. He peered up at Dave through them. "You're some kind of cop, no? I saw you with them on the beach. I heard you tell Bambi O'Mara you didn't think Lily killed Robinson." Dieterle cocked his head. "You think Bambi did it?"

"Why would I think that?"

"Hell, she was in love with Robinson. And I mean, off the deep end. Weird, a smart chick like that. Not to mention her looks. You know she was a *Playboy* centerfold?"

"It's raining and I'm getting wet," Dave said. "Tell me why she'd kill Robinson so I can go get Slocum to put cuffs on her."

Dieterle's mouth fell open. "Ah, now, wait. I didn't mean to get her in trouble. I figured you knew." He blinked anxious through the glasses. "Anybody around here could have told you. She made a spectacle of herself." Maybe the word reminded him. He took off the horn-rims, poked in the dash for a Kleenex, wiped the rain off the lenses. "I mean, what chance did she have?" He dropped the tissues on the floor and put the glasses back on. "Robinson was a fag, worked in a fag bar. It didn't faze her. So many chicks like that—figure one good lay with them and a flit will forget all about boys. Except Bambi never got the lay. And Robinson got Ed Lily. And did she hate Lily! Hoo!"

"And so she shot Robinson dead." Dave straightened, looked away to where rain glazed cars hissed past against the rain curtained background of another cliff. "Hell hath no fury, et cetera?"

"And framed Lily for it. You follow?"

"Thanks," Dave said. "I'll check her out."

"Any time." Dieterle reached and turned the key and the engine started with a snarl. "What'd I tell you?" he yelled. The car backed, scattering wet gravel, swung in a bucking U, and headed down the highway toward Surf. Fast. Dave watched. Being in a chronic hurry must be rough on a man who couldn't stop talking.

Nobody ate at The Big Cup because it was an openfront place and rain was lashing its white Formica. It faced a broad belt of cement that marked off the seedy shops and scabby apartment buildings of Venice from the beach where red dune fences leaned. Dave got coffee in an outsize cup and took it into a phone booth. After a swallow of coffee, he lit a cigarette and dialled people he knew in the television business. He didn't learn anything but they'd be able to tell him later.

He returned the empty mug to the empty counter and hiked a block among puddles to the Billy Budd whose neon sign buzzed and sputtered as if rain had leaked into it. He checked his watch.

Twenty minutes ago it had been noon. A yellowed card tacked to the black door said in faded felt pen that the hours were 12 noon to 2 A.M. But the door was padlocked. He put on reading glasses and bent to look for an emergency number on the card and a voice back of him said:

"Excuse me."

The voice belonged to a bony man, a boy of fifty, in an expensive raincoat and expensive cologne. He was out of breath, pale, and when he used a key on the padlock, his hands shook. He pushed open the door and bad air came out—stale cigarette smoke, last night's spilled whiskey. He kicked a rubber wedge under the door to hold it open and went inside.

Dave followed. The place was dark but he found the bar that had a padded leather bevel for the elbows and padded leather stools that sighed. Somewhere at the back, a door opened and fell shut. Fluorescent tubing winked on behind the bar, slicking mirrors, glinting on rows of bottles, stacks of glasses. A motor whined, fan blades clattered, air began to blow along the room. The man came out without his raincoat, without his suitcoat. The shirt was expensive too. But he'd sweated it.

"Weather, right? What can I get you?"

"Just the answer to a question," Dave said. "What did you want at Arthur Thomas Robinson's apartment in Surf this morning?"

The man narrowed his lovely eyes. "Who are you?"

Dave told him. "There are details the police haven't time for. I've got time. Can I have your answer?"

"Will you leave without it? No—I didn't think so."
The man turned away to drop ice into glasses. He
tilted in whiskey, edged in water. He set a glass in
front of Dave, held one himself. The shaking of
his hand made the ice tinkle. The sound wasn't
Christmasy. "All right," he said. "Let's see if I can
shock you. Ten years ago, Arthur Thomas Robinson and I were lovers."

"You don't shock me," Dave said. "But it's not
responsive to my question."

"I wrote him letters. I wanted those letters back
before his oh-so-righteous brother got his hands on
them. I didn't know how to go about it. I simply
drove over to Robbie's. I mean—I never see television. What do I know about police procedure?"

"Ten years ago," Dave said. "Does that mean
Robinson left you for Bruce K. Shevel?"

"That evil mummy," the man said.

"Clear up something for me." Dave tried the
whiskey. Rich and smooth. They didn't serve this
out of the well. "Shevel said he'd met Robinson in
the hospital. Robinson was an orderly. A neighbor
named Bambi O'Mara says Robinson was a bar-
keep all his life."

The man nodded. "I taught him all he knew. He
was eighteen when he drifted in here." The man's
eyes grew wet. He turned away and lit a cigarette.
"He'd never had another job in his life. Orderly?
Be serious! He fainted at the sight of blood. No,
one sinister night Bruce Shevel walked in here,
slumming. And that was the beginning of the end.
An *old* man. He was, even then. He must be all
glamour by now."

"You know that Robinson kept your letters?"

"Yes. He was always promising to return them but he didn't get around to it. Now he never will." The man's voice broke and he took a long swallow from his drink. "That damn brother will probably have apoplexy when he reads them. And of course he'll read them. His type are always snooping after sin. Claim it revolts them but they can't get enough. And of course, he hated me. Always claimed I'd perverted his baby brother. We had some pretty ugly dialogs when he found out Robbie and I were sleeping together. I wouldn't put it past him to go to the liquor board with those letters. You've got to have unimpeachable morals to run a bar, you know. It could be the end of me."

"I don't think he's that kind of hater," Dave said. "Are you Lauder?"

"I'm White, Wilbur White. Bob Lauder and I have been partners since we got out of the Army— World War II. We've had bars all over L. A. County. Fifteen years here in Venice."

"Where is he now?"

"Bob? He'll be in at six. Today's my long day. His was yesterday. It's getting exhausting. We haven't replaced Robbie yet." He tried for a wan smile. "Of course we never will. But we'll hire somebody."

"You live in Venice?" Dave asked.

"Oh, heavens, no. Malibu."

It was a handsome new place on the beach. Raw cedar planking. An Alfa Romeo stood in the carport. Dave pulled the company car into the empty space beside it. The house door was a slab at the far end of a walk under a flat roof overhang. He worked a bell push. Bob Lauder was a time getting to the door. When he opened it he was in a bathrobe and a bad mood. He was as squat and pudgy as his partner was the opposite. His scant hair was tousled, his eyes were pouchy. He winced at the daylight, what there was of it.

"Sorry to bother you," Dave said. "But I'm death claims investigator for Medallion Life. Arthur Robinson was insured with us. He worked for you. Can I ask you a few questions?"

"The police asked questions yesterday," Lauder said.

"The police don't care about my company's ten thousand dollars," Dave said. "I do."

"Come in, stay out, I don't give a damn." Lauder flopped a hand and turned away. "All I want is sleep."

It was Dave's day for livingrooms facing the Pacific. Lauder dropped onto a couch and leaned forward, head in hands, moaning quietly to himself.

"I've heard," Dave said, "that Robinson was good for business, that you were happy to get him back."

"He was good for business," Lauder droned.

"But you weren't happy to get him back?"

"Wilbur was happy." Lauder looked up, red-eyed. "Wilbur was overjoyed. Wilbur came un-God-dam—glued."

"To the extent of letting Robinson take what he wanted from the till?"

"How did you know? We didn't tell the police."

Dave shrugged. "He was hurting for money."

"Yeah. Wilbur tried to cover for him. I let him think it worked. But I knew." He rose and tottered off. "I need some coffee."

Dave went after him, leaned in a kitchen doorway and watched him heat a pottery urn of leftover coffee on a bricked-in burner deck. "How long have you and Wilbur been together?"

"Thirty years"—Lauder reached down a mug from a hook—"since you ask."

"Because you didn't let the Arthur Thomas Robinsons of this world break it up, right? There were others, weren't there?"

"You don't look it, you don't sound it, but you have got to be gay. Nobody straight could guess that." Lauder peered into the mouth of the pot, hoping for steam. "Yes. It wasn't easy but it was worth it. To me. If you met Wilbur, you'd see why."

Dave didn't. "Do you own a hunting rifle? Say a thirty-thirty?"

Lauder turned and squinted. "What does that mean? Look, I was working in the bar when Robbie got it. I did not get jealous and kill him, if that's what you're thinking. Or did I do it to stop him skimming fifty bucks an evening off the take?"

"I'm trying to find out what to think," Dave said.

"Try someplace else." Lauder forgot to wait for the steam. He set the mug down hard and sloshed coffee into it. "Try now. Get out of here."

"If you bought a rifle in the past five-six years," Dave said, "there'll be a Federal registration record."

"We own a little pistol," Lauder said. "We keep it at the bar. Unloaded. To scare unruly trade."

Where Los Santos canyon did a crooked fall out of tree-green hills at the coast road was a cluster of Tudor style buildings whose 1930 stucco fronts looked mushy in the rain. Between a shop that sold snorkles and swim-fins and a hamburger place Dave remembered from his childhood lurked three telephone booths. Two were occupied by women in flowered plastic raincoats and hair curlers, trying to let somebody useful know their cars had stalled. He took the third booth and dialled the television people again.

While he learned that Bambi O'Mara had definitely been in Bear Paw, Montana, at the time a bullet made a clean hole through the skull of the man she loved, Dave noticed a scabby sign across the street above a door with long black iron hinges. L. DIETERLE REAL ESTATE. He glanced along the street for the battered Triumph. It wasn't in sight but it could be back of the building. He'd see later. Now he phoned Lieutenant Ken Barker.

He was at his desk. Still. Or again. "Dave?"

"Shevel is lying. He wouldn't lie for no reason."

"Your grammar shocks me," Barker said.

"He claims he met Robinson when he was in the hospital. *After* his so-called accident. Says Robinson was an orderly. But at the Sea Shanty they say Shevel *walked* in one night and met Robinson. According to a girlfriend, Robinson was never anything but a bartender. You want to check Junipero Hospital's employment records?"

"For two reasons," Barker said. "First, that rifle didn't have any prints on it and it was bought long before Congress ordered hunting guns registered. Second, an hour ago the Coast Guard rescued a kid in a power boat getting battered on the rocks off Point Placentia. It wasn't his power boat. It's registered to one Bruce K. Shevel. The kid works at the Marina. My bet is he was heading for Mexico."

"Even money," Dave said. "His name is Manuel—right? Five foot six, a hundred twenty pounds, long hair? Somewhere around twenty?"

"You left out something," Barker said. "He's scared to death. He won't say why, but it's not just about what happened to the boat. I'll call Junipero."

"Thanks," Dave said. "I'll get back to you."

He left the booth and dodged rain-bright bumpers to the opposite curb. He took a worn step up and pushed the real estate office door. Glossy eight by tens of used Los Santos and Surf side street bungalows curled on the walls. A scarred desk was piled with phone directories. They slumped against a finger smeared telephone. A nameplate by the telephone said *L. Dieterle*. But the little man wasn't in the chair back of the desk.

The room wasn't big to start with but a Masonite partition halved it and behind this a typewriter rattled. A lumberyard bargain door was shut at the end of the partition. Tacked to the door was a pasteboard dimestore sign NOTARY and under it a business card. *Verna Marie Casper, Public Stenographer*. He rapped the door and a tin voice told him to come in.

She'd used henna on her hair for a lot of years. Her makeup too was like Raggedy Ann's. Including the yarn eyelashes. She was sixty but the dress was off the Young Misses rack at Grant's. Glass diamonds sparked at her ears, her scrawny throat, her wrists, the bony hands that worked a Selectric with a finish like a Negev tank. She wasn't going to, but he said anyway:

"Don't let me interrupt you. I just want to know when Mr. Dieterle will be back."

"Can't say," she said above the fast clatter of the type ball. "He's in and out. A nervous man, very nervous. You didn't miss him by long. He was shaking today. That's a new one."

"He thinks the storm is going to knock down his apartments in Surf," Dave said. "Will you take a message for him?"

"What I write down I get paid for," she said. "He was going through phone books. So frantic he tore pages. Really. Look"—suddenly she stopped typing and stared at Dave—"I just sublet this space. We're not in business together. He looks after his business. I look after mine. I'm self-sufficient."

"Get a lot of work, do you?"

"I'm part of this community," she said and began typing again. "A valued part. They gave me a testimonial dinner at the Chamber of Commerce last fall. Forty years of loyal public service."

"I believe it," Dave said. "Ever do anything for a man named Robinson? Recently, say—the last two weeks or so? Arthur Thomas Robinson?"

She broke off typing again and eyed him fiercely. "Are you a police officer? Are you authorized to have such information?"

"He wanted you to write out an affidavit for him, didn't he?" Dave said. "And to notarize it?"

"Now, see here! You know I can't—"

"I'm not asking what was in it. I think I know. I also think it's what got him killed."

"Killed!" She went white under the circles of

rouge. "But he only did it to clear his conscience! He said—" She clapped a hand to her mouth and glared at Dave. "You! You're trying to trick me. Well, it won't work. What I'm told is strictly confidential."

Dave swung away. His knuckles rapped the Masonite as he went out of her cubbyhole. "Not with this partition," he said. "With Dieterle on the other side."

Past batting windshield wipers, he saw the steeple down the block above the dark greenery of old acacia trees. Merwin Robinson had told the truth about the neighborhood. Old one story frame houses with weedy front yards where broken down autos turned to rust. Stray dogs ran cracked sidewalks in the rain. An old woman in man's shoes and hat dragged a coaster wagon through puddles.

CHURCH OF GOD'S ABUNDANCE was what the weathered signboard said. God's neglect was what showed. Dave tried the front doors from which the yellow varnish was peeling. They were loose in their frame but locked. A hollow echo came back from the rattling he gave them. He followed a narrow strip of cement that led along the shingled side of the church to a shingle-sided bungalow at the rear. The paint flaking off it was the same as what flaked off the church, white turning yellow. There was even a cloverleaf of stained glass in the door. *Rev. Merwin Robinson* in time dimmed ink was in a little brass frame above a bell push.

But the buzz pushing it made at the back of the

house brought nobody. A dented gray and blue sedan with fifties tail fins stood at the end of the porch. Its trunk was open. Some of Arthur Thomas Robinson's clothes were getting rained on. Dave tried the tongue latch of the house door and it opened. He put his head inside, called for the preacher. It was dusky in the house. No lights anywhere. Dave stepped inside onto a threadbare carpet held down by overstuffed chairs covered in faded chintz.

"Reverend Robinson?"

No answer. He moved past a room divider of built-in bookcases with diamond-pane glass doors. There was a round golden oak diningroom table under a chain—suspended stained-glass light fixture. Robinson evidently used the table as a desk. Books were stacked on it. A loose leaf binder lay open, a page half filled with writing in ballpoint. *Am I my brother's keeper?* Sermon topic. But not for this week. Not for any week now.

Because on the far side of the table, by a kitchen swing door his head had pushed ajar when he fell, Merwin Robinson lay on his back and stared at Dave with the amazed eyes of the dead. One of his hands clutched something white. Dave knelt. It was an envelope, torn open, empty. But the stamp hadn't been cancelled. He put on his glasses, flicked his lighter to read the the address. *City Attorney, 200 Spring St., Los Angeles, CA.* Neatly typed on an electric machine with carbon ribbon. Probably the battered IBM in Verna Casper's office.

Which meant there wasn't time to hunt up the rectory phone in the gloom, to report, to explain. It didn't matter. Merwin Robinson wouldn't be any deader an hour from now. But somebody else might be, unless Dave got back to the beach. Fast.

Wind lashed rain across the expensive decks of the apartments facing the Marina. It made the wet trenchcoat clumsy, flapping around his legs. Then he quit running because he saw the door. He took the last yards in careful, soundless steps. The door was shut. That would be reflex even for a man in a chronic hurry—to shut out the storm. And that man had to be here. The Triumph was in the lot.

Dave put a hand to the cold, wet brass knob. It turned. He leaned gently against the door. It opened. He edged in and softly shut it. The same yammering voice he'd heard earlier today in Surf above the wash of rain and tide, yammered now someplace beyond the climbing vines.

"—That you got him to help you try to rip off an insurance company—accident and injury. By knocking your car off the jack while one wheel was stripped and your foot was under it. And he told you he was going to spill the whole story unless you paid out."

"I'm supposed to believe it's on that paper?" Shevel's voice came from just the other side of the philodendrons. "That Robbie actually—"

"Yeah, right—he dictated it to the old hag that's a notary public, splits my office space with me. I heard it all. He told her he'd give you twenty-four hours to cop out too, then he'd mail it. But I didn't think it was a clear conscience he was after. He was after money—for a sportscar for that hustler he was keeping."

"I'm surprised at Robbie," Shevel said. "He often threatened to do things. He rarely did them."

"He did this. And you knew he would. Only how did you waste him? You can't get out of that chair."

"I had two plans. The other was complicated—a bomb in his car. Happily, the simpler plan worked out. It was a lovely evening. The storm building up off the coast made for a handsome sunset. The sea was calm—long, slow swells. I decided to take an hour's cruise in my launch. I have a young friend who skippers it for me."

"You shot him from out there?"

"The draft is shallow. Manuel was able to steer quite close in. It can't have been a hundred fifty yards. Robbie was on the deck as I'd expected. It was warm, and he adored sunsets with his martinis. Manuel's a fine marksman. Twenty four months in Viet Nam sharpened his natural skills. And the gun was serviceable." Shevel's voice went hard. "This gun is not, but you're too close to miss. Hand over that paper. No, don't try anything. I warn you—"

Dave stepped around the screen of vines and chopped at Shevel's wrist. The gun went off with a slapping sound. The rug furrowed at Dieterle's feet. Shevel screamed rage, struggled in the wheelchair, clawed at Dave's eyes. Dieterle tried to run past. Dave put a foot in his way. He sprawled. Dave wrenched the .22 out of Shevel's grip, leveled it at them, backed to a white telephone, cranked zero and asked an operator to get him the police.

Ken Barker had managed a shower and a shave. He still looked wearier than this morning. But he worked up a kind of smile. "Neat," he said. "You think like a machine—a machine that gets the company's money back."

"Shevel's solvent but not that solvent," Dave said. "Hell, we paid out a hundred thousand initially. I don't remember what the monthly payments were. We'll be lucky to get half. And we'll have to sue for that." He frowned at a paper in his hands, typing on a police form, signed in shaky ballpoint—*Manuel Sanchez*. It said Shevel had done the shooting. He, Manuel, had only run the boat. "Be sure this kid gets a good lawyer."

"The best in the Public Defender's office."

"No." Dave rose, flapped into the trenchcoat. "Not good enough. Medallion will foot the bill. I'll send Abe Greenglass. Tomorrow morning."

"Jesus." Barker blinked. "Remind me never to cross you."

Dave grinned, worked the coat's wet leather buttons, quit grinning. "I'm sorry about Robinson's brother. If I'd just been a little quicker—"

"It was natural causes," Barker said. "Don't blame yourself. Can't even blame Dieterle—or Wilbur White."

"The bar owner? You mean he was there?"

"Slocum checked him out. He had the letters."

"Yup." Dave fastened the coat belt. "Twenty minutes late to work. White, sweaty, shaking. It figures. Hell, he even talked about apoplexy, how the Reverend hated him for perverting his brother."

"The man had horrible blood pressure," Barker said. "We talked to his doctor. He'd warned him.

The least excitement and"—Barker snapped his fingers—"cerebral hemorrhage. Told him to retire. Robinson refused. They needed him—the people at that run-down church."

"It figures," Dave said. "He didn't make it easy, but he was the only one in this mess I could like. A little."

"Not Bambi O'Mara?" Barker went and snagged a topcoat from a rack. "She looked great in those magazine spreads." He took Dave's arm, steered him between gray-green desks toward a gray-green door. "I want to hear all about her. I'll buy you a drink."

But the phone rang and called him back. And Dave walked alone out of the beautiful, bright glass building into the rain that looked as if it would never stop falling.

Willow's Money

She backed the heavy car twice before she got it straight in the slot marked with her name in the parking level under the apartment building. The long, red hood of the car sloped away at its front, so she couldn't see its limits. Also, it was hard for her to steer. Her choice would have been a light, upright little Japanese car with square, visible corners.

The Corvette was hers, bought with her money, but Mabel had chosen it. Mabel had driven it, jaw thrust out, pudgy fists tight on the leather-wrapped steering wheel, a grim chuckle in her throat, as if she held the reins of strong, unruly horses. She could whip into this narrow parking space without trouble. But that was before her back had crippled her at last. Now she never drove, and Willow was stuck with the car.

She got out and locked it. In the late night emptiness of the parking level, the jingle of her keys was loud. Willow never gave it a thought, but Mabel fretted about this place after dark. The lighting came feebly from fluorescent tubes spaced far apart in a line down the middle of the ceiling. Edges and corners lay in shadow. Muggers could be lurking. Rapists. Mabel feared terrible things would happen to Willow down here alone, and she tried to keep her from going out at night.

Smiling wanly to herself, Willow slid her key into the stairwell doorknob, opened the door, and there was Mabel with the gun. She sat on the lowest of the cement steps, asleep, chin on her chest, a hand on the gun in her lap, a fat old woman with short-cropped gray hair, and dressed in blue jeans and a sweatshirt. Willow closed her eyes and opened them again.

"Mabel," she said. "For God's sake."

Mabel awoke with a start, and the gun bounced off a step and skidded to Willow's feet. The clatter of it echoed up the stairwell. Mabel started to lunge for the gun and fell back onto the step with a cry. Sudden moves could send stabs of pain into the small of her back. She said, "Where the hell have you been? Do you know what time it is?"

"What are you doing down here?" Willow looked at her watch. "It isn't even eleven."

"You left at seven." Mabel clutched the steel pipe stair rail and, wincing, dragged herself to her feet. "It got later and later. I pictured you lying down here knocked over the head or worse. I had to come down, didn't I?"

Willow crouched and picked up the gun, cold and heavy and black. "If a robber saw you with this, he'd kill you on the spot. Your back will be a wreck for a week, sitting that way."

"I'd blow his black head off," Mabel said.

"He might not be black," Willow said, knowing it was useless. "Why wouldn't he be Swedish?"

Mabel snorted and turned to climb the stairs. "So," she said, going painfully, slowly, a step at a time, leading always with her right foot in its worn tennis shoe, "what did he have to say? Must have been fascinating to hold you spellbound for three hours."

"He loves to talk." Willow dropped the gun into her shoulder bag and ran lightly up the steps to take Mabel's arm and help her climb. "He seemed to really want me to stay. I didn't want to offend him. How would that help?"

"It's a good script," Mabel said. "You didn't have to walk on eggs." They reached the landing. She was pale. "Let's wait here a minute, okay? Have you got a cigarette?" Willow dug her pack from the shoulder bag and lit cigarettes for both of them. "Damn left leg." Cigarette hanging tough from a corner of her mouth, she bent to rub the leg. "Giving out on me completely tonight."

"You could lose a little weight," Willow said.

"What am I supposed to do—take up jogging?"

Willow sighed. "You could cut back on the beer." She glanced down the stairs. No sign of a Coor's can. Mabel was never without one in her hand, from breakfast to bedtime. Nor was she often without a cigarette. Had she really been so worried tonight that she'd forgotten both? Willow felt a rush of guilt and gratitude. She would never get used to how her welfare was always on Mabel's mind. Willow's parents had never been like that. "You know how it puts on the pounds."

"When I need a sermon on drinking from you," Mabel said, "I'll let you know."

Willow flinched. It wasn't fair. She had never taken a drink in her young life before she met Mabel. How was she to know she couldn't handle alcohol? And it hadn't been beer, then, either. It had been Manhattans or Daiquiris before lunch,

Martinis before dinner, wine with dinner, brandy after dinner, Scotch all evening long. Why not? They were celebrating the miracle of their having met, and their astonished joy at being together without a worry in the world, without another soul to answer to, day and night, forever and ever.

They were celebrating Willow's money, and all the lovely things it could buy, the apartment, the car, the trips to San Francisco, Hawaii, Mazatlan, New Orleans, the jet flights, the wonderful restaurants, the handsome hotel rooms high up in glass towers with the blue sea sparkling below. Willow thought they were drunk on happiness. It came as a shock to learn that they were simply drunk, a couple of staggering, stupefied, food-spilling, mumbling, giggling, falling-down wretches, unable to help themselves or each other.

A Highway Patrol car stopped them on an empty two A.M. highway to Palm Springs, the Corvette hurtling along through the glass-black desert night at ninety miles an hour, Mabel at the wheel, roaring with laughter, Willow clutching a bottle in a smiling daze. In those times, Mabel took sudden notions—let's go here, let's go there. What the clock said, the weather outside, the day of the week, didn't matter. To pick up when you wanted to and simply go where you felt like going was freedom she couldn't get enough of. It exhilerated Willow too.

Then suddenly this freedom slowed down, bumped with drumming tires along the rough road shoulder, and lurched to a halt. A flashlight glared in their faces. An unshaven, middle-aged man in knife-creased suntans yawned while he questioned them and filled out forms. He rubbed his belly against Willow while he took her fingerprints. His breath was stale. They were locked into a cell with shiny bars, where the toilet had no seat. The air smelled of vomit, urine, and disinfectant, and there was no way to turn off the lightbulb in its ceiling cage.

Mabel fell heavily asleep, mouth open, drooling, snoring, on the thin gray mattress of a steel bunk hinged to the wall. Willow, feeling cold sober for the first time in months, a year, more than a year, paced the graypainted cement floor, head throbbing, mouth dry and sour, waiting for Billy Nettles to come. He was her dead father's lawyer, a tall, lanky, big-eared man whose clothes were always rumpled. As she quavered weepily to him over the Highway Patrol's office phone, she wished this were a dream. It wasn't. A dream was what she'd been living in till now.

It was eleven o'clock before they walked out into sunlight and fresh air. Billy Nettles had not come. He had sent his son, Nash. Nash was as neat as his father was dishevelled. He insisted on driving Willow back to Los Angeles, leaving Mabel to return alone in the Corvette. Mabel was pale, sick, shaking. "Never another God damn drink," she kept muttering to Willow while judge, officers, lawyer, arranged for their release in a bare, sand-color courtroom. But as Willow watched her drive away, she knew that at the first tavern she saw, Mabel would stop to steady her nerves and settle her stomach with brandies.

Sure enough, before Nash's new Mercedes reached the edge of town, Willow spotted the red Corvette in a dusty parkinglot beside a scaly stucco place called the Hitching Post. She shouldn't, but Willow felt a pang of envy for Mabel. Nash didn't notice the car. He was busy being stern with Willow. He wasn't much older than she. They'd played together as children. But that didn't stop him. "Dad wanted to put that insurance payment in a trust fund. He said you weren't old enough to handle that kind of money. Looks like he was right. Who is that woman? What were you doing with her? Don't you have any friends your own age?"

"People my own age," Willow said, "are boring."

"As boring as some fat, drunken, old bulldyke?"

Willow felt slapped. She bit her lip. Tears stung her eyes. She turned her face away and watched the desert pass, the flat, gritty land, the dry, bleachy scrub, the occasional lonely Joshua tree. She waited until the shock of his words wore off. She looked at him. He was delicately beautiful, with his neatly trimmed little beard and mustache, his handmade shirt, tailored pinstripe suit, Rolex watch on a slender wrist. She asked:

"Do you know why my father cut me out of his will?"

Nash said, "You're in his will. If you marry and have children, you get a quarter of a million dollars."

"I told him I would never do that."

"Never is a long time," Nash said.

"I am a thin, drunken, young calfdyke," Willow said. "But he wouldn't accept that. He thought he could bribe me out of it. Money can't change the color of a person's eyes."

Nash used his father's Texas twang. "It shore can smooth a bumpy trail." He threw her a quick frown. "Was that why you always beat me at tennis?"

"Are you gay?" Willow asked.

He shook his head. "Just bad at tennis," he said. "You were used to money. How did you like it, having to drudge for a paycheck? Advertising agency, wasn't it?"

"Publications," Willow said. "I didn't like it. I don't have any training to do anything useful in a place like that. Or anywhere. I can't even type. Someone like that, anyone can order around. It was no fun. But that's where I met Mabel. She is not an old drunk. She is a very gifted writer, and I admire her very much, and I am"—Willow was afraid she was going to start to cry, and she swallowed and blinked—"I am honored every day of my life that she wants me for her friend."

"Willow"—he spoke the name with that patronizing boredom he had used on her when he was twelve and she was nine—"very gifted writers don't work in advertising agencies. People who dream they're going to be writers someday work in advertising agencies."

"It wasn't an advertising agency," Willow shouted. "I told you—it was publications."

"What does that mean? She wrote fix-it-yourself columns for *Diesel Digest*?"

"She was an editor," Willow said hotly. "And a

very good one. Everyone in the place came to her for advice. They offered to double her salary to make her stay."

"But she didn't stay, did she?" Nash's slim hand tinkered with the air conditioning controls on the dash. "That Corvette is yours, but she was driving it. Does she use your bed the same way?"

Willow turned sharply from him and groped for the door handle. "Stop this car. I'm not going any farther with you."

Nash only raised his neat, very dark, dense eyebrows. He didn't stop the car. He didn't even slow it. "Her address is the same as yours. You're keeping her—isn't that how it is?"

"She needed time and freedom to write," Willow said. "I could give her that. I had plenty of money."

"A hundred fifty thousand from the two policies," Nash said. Willow's father had crashed his Cessna in a pine-grown Wyoming wilderness. Her mother had been the only passenger. "That's not a bad sum, if you invested it wisely. My father told you that." Nash leaned across her to get glasses from the glove compartment. "Did you invest it?" He hooked the glasses over his ears and glanced at her through the mirror lenses. He looked like a South American torturer. "You didn't, did you?" Willow stared ahead at the unswerving strip of highway. Nash said, "As I understand these things, if you want to master an art, painting, music, writing, you spend half a lifetime just getting the skills down. How old is she, exactly? She doesn't walk young."

"She has a slipped disc," Willow said. "That was

another reason I couldn't leave her in that office. Sitting at a desk all day—the pressures, the tensions—she was in agony."

"She wasn't feeling any pain last night," Nash said. "Not according to the arrest report. Haig and Haig's quite a relaxant. Doesn't it make her writing a little blurry?"

"She's doing a marvelous screenplay," Willow said. "She has friends in the picture business, and all of them say it's a sure thing."

"But it's not finished, right?" Nash said.

Willow felt her face turn red. "You don't hurry creative people. That's not how artists work."

"She's conning you, Willow," Nash said. "You hungry? This looks passable." He wheeled the Mercedes into a freshly blacktopped parking lot beside a restaurant of white painted brick, raftered eaves, stained glass. Willow felt abused and sulky. She didn't want to eat with him. She sat in the car when he got out. He peered in at her. She said:

"What's Mrs. Nettles going to say about you having lunch with another woman?"

He looked surprised. "My mother?"

"Your wife," she said.

He laughed. "Get out. Junior law partners don't have time for wives."

She got out reluctantly into the stunning blaze of sun and heat. She trailed glumly after him across the tarmac, feeling grubby, the smell of the jail still in her nostrils. She wasn't fit to go into a nice place. But her heartbeat quickened when they stepped inside, and she saw bottles glinting in the air-conditioned shadows, and smelled bourbon, and heard the tinkle of ice. Nash took off the mirror lenses and looked at her inquiringly. "You were pretty juiced last night. Would a drink make you feel better?"

She raised her chin. "No, thank you," she said, and walked quickly toward the diningroom.

Now, on the bleak landing of the stairwell, she dropped her cigarette and stepped on it. "I'm not going to give you a sermon on drinking." She took Mabel's arm again. "I only want you to feel better, is all. When you're in pain, I'm in pain—all right?"

"I can quit any time I want to." Mabel gripped the steel hand rail and, grunting, began to climb again. "And I don't need a roomful of sanctimonious ex-drunks to help me." She was sure Willow talked about her at Alcoholics Anonymous meetings, blaming Mabel for turning her into a drunk. Also, Mabel had it fixed in her head that AA had something to do with God, and she hated God for having made her a man in a woman's body. She never wasted a chance to dig at Willow about AA. Willow had given up answering back. Mabel said, "I finished the script, didn't I? Laid off the hard stuff for seven months. What more do you want from me?"

"I'm proud of you, and I'm proud of the script." The gun in the shoulder bag thumped Willow's hip. She was going to have a bruise there. "Gil Berger is going to love it. He's witty. He'll understand your humor."

"He'd better love it," Mabel grumbled. "He's our last chance, kiddo."

To hear Mabel tell it, her friends in the picture business were people with power. It turned out, they were nobodies—plump, frog-mouthed, effeminate Dorsey, an assistant set decorator; frantic, frizzy-haired Katrina with the staring eyes, who did renderings in the costume department; and Boy, a reedy tough girl from Arkansas who ran multigraphs in the script department. When Willow at last learned who they were, from a drunk and red-faced Mabel after the last of them had let her down, she was shocked. She didn't know whether to laugh or cry at the spectacle of Mabel cursing and kicking the yellow-covered scripts around the room. How could she have put faith in such people? What a waste of time! Willow rescued from a corner the least battered of the scripts. She stood smoothing it against her breast.

"Let me show it to Gil Berger," she said.

"We haven't tried the agencies," Mabel said.

Mabel didn't like Gil Berger, didn't trust him. Berger was a client of Billy Nettles, and when Willow had mentioned to Nash, who, for reasons she couldn't understand, kept taking her to lunch, that Mabel was in trouble with her script and getting no help from the stack of screenwriting handbooks Willow had bought her, Nash wondered why she didn't take a course from Berger who sometimes taught at the University. He was a famous and successful man at his trade. He ought to be able to help.

Mabel resisted. In the first place she would have rejected any suggestion made by Nash because she was jealous of him for paying attention to Willow. Willow only let him buy her expensive lunches because Mabel at the time was boring and bad-tempered, shutting herself away with her typewriter all day and grouchy all evening. She sulked, swore, refused to leave the apartment, even for dinner at the Hungry Hungarian, a little place she loved, with checkered table cloths and candles in Chianti bottles. Willow was careful always to ask if it was all right to go with Nash to lunch, play tennis with Nash, see a film.

"It's your life," Mabel grunted.

She argued against the class. "How can I sit in some crampled little school desk three hours a night? After a day at the typewriter? With my back? Laughable."

"All right," Willow said. "I'll go for you. You write down the questions, and I'll get the answers."

And that was how it was. Berger took a shine to her. A big-bellied, bald, bearded man with a gusty laugh, he didn't fit the Falstaff mold in any other way. He never made a sexual move toward Willow, or uttered a sexual suggestion. He treated her like a boy, and she appreciated that. She loved sitting with him out in a wide, tree-shadowed brick patio at coffee-break time, students with their armloads of books moving in and out of the circles of lamplight—and listening to his funny, self-effacing stories of a long life that seemed to Willow filled with glamour and adventure. She was easy with him.

Easy, Mabel was not. She was as jealous of Berger as she was of Nash. And she was strict with Willow. No mention must be made of Mabel to him, and certainly no mention of Mabel's script. Students were supposed to be at work on projects, to show what they'd written to Berger, so he could tell them how to make it better. Mabel refused to let Willow take him so much as a page. "We'll walk into a theatre some night and see it up there on the screen," she said. "We'll switch on the TV, and there my screenplay will be, with his name on it."

"He's not like that," Willow said. "He's been nominated for Academy Awards, for heaven sake. He's won two Emmies. He doesn't need to steal other people's ideas."

"How do you know? How do you know he wrote any of those scripts himself? You don't know that."

So now Willow must waste more weeks trudging from agency to agency, meeting with refusals even to look at the script. Mabel wasn't a member of the Screen Writers Guild. Mabel would never be a member—she despised labor unions. Very grudgingly, always late at night when she was half asleep from all the beer she'd drunk, she began muttering that maybe it would be a good idea to show Gil Berger the script. But when, the next morning, in the sunny kitchen, where Willow always kept fresh flowers on the table, Willow lifted the receiver to call him, Mabel changed her mind.

Nash said, "I know you love her, and you're going to hate me for saying so, but you're wasting your time. It's a no-win proposition, Willow. Writers with long track records in this town are starving while they try to get their stuff in front of the cameras. What hope is there for a complete unknown?"

He was wearing his mirror lenses again. He was being a South American torturer again. Willow looked across the creaky plank deck of the restaurant, across the blue water of the Marina, the sleek white sailboats gently rocking side by side, to the tall new apartment buildings with glinting windows. A jet liner lifted from the faraway airport and took a long, slow curve out over the sea. Her fingers turned the stem of a wine glass in which Perrier water bubbled. She looked at him.

"It's a wonderful, lighthearted script," she said. "It's intelligent and sophisticated. It's the sort of thing the movies used to have and lost. Some producer is going to see it and realise that."

Their lunch came, avocado halves stuffed with shrimp. He said, "Why don't you just take it to Berger on your own?"

"Because"—Willow picked up her fork—"we don't do things behind each others' backs." She took a bite of food. The sun was warm. The cool breeze off the water fluttered her loose organdy blouse. The food was good. "It's a relationship based on trust."

"Before your money runs out completely," Nash said, "why not spend some of it to train yourself for something practical?" He drank some wine. "Take a course in computer programming."

Willow gave a mirthless laugh. "You need to know math for that. I can't add two and two."

"How about word processing?" He chewed. He wiped his neat little beard with his napkin. "Word processers are in great demand."

"I told you, I can't even type."

"Look, I'm not trying to run your life, but you have to face facts. The chances of selling that film script are zilch, Willow. Stop idealizing her. She's about as sophisticated as a tractor. She's crippled, so she can't take a job. What the hell are you going to do? Really. You better learn to add, you better learn to type. You're young, you're not doing anything with your time. You can be whatever you want to be. Only you better get going."

Willow watched the sunlight flare on the petals of geraniums in big pots on the tops of thick pier-stakes that held up the deck. "It would destroy her pride. She'd think I'd lost faith in her. She needs for me to have faith in her, Nash. It's pathetic how badly she needs that. All her life she's wanted to be a writer. All her hopes are in this script. If I go home today and tell her I'm going to train for a job she'll fall apart."

Nash smiled and shook his head sadly. "Oh, Willow, Willow."

"That's from a Shakespeare song," she said. "Are you going to sing me the rest?"

"I forgot my lute," Nash said. He ate the rest of his lunch, sipping wine between bites, then touched his beard with the napkin again, and laid the napkin beside his plate. He lit a cigarette and leaned back in the bentwood chair. "Okay," he said. "Try Saxon-Reeves."

She scoffed. "You have to be Harold Robbins, Sidney Sheldon, Robert Ludlum."

"You don't remember Kirk Saxon? He was one of your father's clients. He was a friend. I used to see him at your house all the time."

Willow had a dim picture of a chubby man with tiny feet and hands, ruddy cheeks, baby blue eyes. She smelled linament, and the sweet smoke of expensive, slim cigars. Kirk Saxon. Once, dressed in crisp summer whites, he had tried to show her how to hit a badminton bird with a racquet almost as big as she was. "I'd forgotten," she said. "Will he remember me?"

"You were the prettiest little thing that ever lived," Nash said. "You still are. What about dessert?"

Kirk Saxon was dead. Willow must have looked stricken. That was how she felt. Not for Mr. Saxon, whom she scarcely remembered, but for Mabel, Mabel's script, Mabel's hopes. Willow ought not to have been so gleeful, so filled with hope herself that she couldn't keep her excitement quiet. She might have known it was too good to be true. The Saxon-Reeves receptionist was alarmed, solicitous, kind. She sent Willow to see the Pink Pig.

"No problem," said the Pink Pig, with a little feral smile. She patted the script on her desk. "I'll see to it that Mr. Reeves himself reads this. I'll see that it gets top priority." Willow felt a rush of joy that made her dizzy. Then the Pink Pig grew business-like and confidential. In order to bring the promised miracle to pass, she would need five hundred dollars in cash. In a plain envelope. Handed to her tomorrow, at lunch, in a restaurant she named, a restaurant far across town.

Not even remembering to snatch up the script, Willow rushed from the room. She fluttered up and down the panelled hallways of the agency, looking for a door marked Norman Reeves. Music drifted in the air. Big abstract paintings smiled at her. She couldn't find the door. Out of breath, ready to cry, she stopped at last. It was no use. If she found his office, would his secretary let her pass? If she did, would he believe Willow? Why? She had no proof. She thought crazily of meeting the Pink Pig at the restaurant tomorrow, taking along hidden in her shoulder bag the cassette recorder Mabel sometimes dictated into. But that was the stuff of television cop shows. They made it look easy. But she'd be sure to fumble, trying to turn the machine on, and the Pink Pig would realize what she was up to. Head lowered, feet scuffing in the worn sandals she'd paid so much for long ago on Rodeo Drive, she hurried across the deep-carpeted reception room with its lush plantings and brown velveteen couches and chairs, and let an elevator whisper her back to earth.

"What!" Mabel, clothed except for shoes, lay propped on pillows, a pillow under her knees as the doctor had prescribed. She had her can of beer. Two empty ones lay on the floor. The bedroom was foggy with cigarette smoke, the ashtray clogged with butts. She was reading an old Agatha Christie in a paperback copy falling apart. She favored books from the past. The new ones had no plots and were filled with senseless violence and filth. She threw the book at the closet door and struggled, red-faced, to get out of bed. "Why the hell didn't you ask the receptionist where his office was? Why didn't you tell her what happened?" She stuck her feet into her special hundred-dollar orthopedic loafers, and kicked the beer cans out of the way. "That's a reputable agency. They're not going to let that kind of thing go on." She heaved herself upright and rummaged in the drawer of the bedside table. The lampshade quivered. She brought out the gun and stuck it in the waistband of her jeans, which were crumpled and not quite clean. "Get out of my way." She barged at Willow in the door. "I'll soon fix this. Proof?" With a sour laugh, she thrust Willow aside. Lumbering down the hallway, she said, "When I stick a gun in her face, she'll give him proof. Imagine that bitch! Thinking she could get away with it. She sure had you sized up, didn't she? No guts." Mabel was in the kitchen, glaring furiously around. "Where are the God damned car keys? I'll show her guts."

"Mabel, give me that silly gun. You're not going down there waving a gun around." She advanced on Mabel, holding out a hand. "The men in white will come for you."

"When Reeves finds out what happened"—Mabel knocked Willow's hand away and backed off—"he'll have to read the script. Only decent thing he can do."

"If you go in there roaring like Rooster Cogburn with six-guns ablaze," Willow said, "he'll think you're crazy. Why would he read a crazy woman's script?"

"Hah! Now it comes out." Mabel stood leaning back against a counter, flushed, breathing hard. "You think I'm bonkers." Mabel used British expressions when reading Agatha Christie. "You think it's a crazy woman's script. You never believed in it. You never believed in me. That's why you didn't try today. That's why you never tried. You're ashamed of me. You think I'm crazy."

"Mabel, stop. You're hysterical. You don't know what you're saying. Now, give me that." Willow grabbed the butt of the gun and yanked it free. Mabel lunged for it. Willow danced lightly aside, holding it high. Mabel glowered, tucking in her shirt tail. Willow said, "We'll just forget Norman Reeves. We don't need him. We certainly don't need him with a bullet hole in him."

"It wasn't him I was going to shoot," Mabel said. "I was going to shoot that Pink Pig."

"Let it be." Willow went to put away the gun. She laid it back in the bed stand drawer, then frowned and took it out again. She emptied the bullets from the chamber. Then she left the gun in the drawer. The bullets she tucked under some clothes in a bottom dresser drawer. She was deathly afraid of the gun. She ought to put it out with the trash next week. But she didn't have the guts. Mabel sat on a rattan stool at the bar in the livingroom. She was smoking a cigarette, a highball glass almost full of neat whiskey was in her other hand. She was staring out at the sunlit city below, the red roofs among green treetops, the flicker of glare off the glass and metal of moving cars. Willow said, "We've wasted too much time. Whether you like it or not, I'm taking that script to Gil Berger." She picked up the receiver, and this time Mabel didn't stop her when she punched Berger's number. The phone was answered on the first ring, and she cried happily, "Hello, Mr. Berger? It's Willow—" But no one was listening. His voice, booming and cordial, was telling anyone who waited to hear the tape on the answering machine that he was in China on a picture and wouldn't be back until September. It was only May.

Now, she opened the door at the top of the stairs from the parking level, and followed hobbling Mabel into a patio where the swimming pool glowed blue in the night, and hidden ground lights made eerily green the big leaves of tropical plants. More stairs remained to be climbed, but she let Mabel rest again, both of them smoking. Soft stereo sounds, television sounds, drifted from the near apartments where the curtains were drawn. Willow felt sad. She loved this place. She didn't want to leave it.

As if Mabel had read her mind, she said, "Kiddo, your Jewboy better do something with that script fast, or we're going to be out on the street." The eyes she turned on Willow in the half dark were those of a frightened child. "Parker stopped me tonight. Right on this spot. Where does she get those pants suits? They look like boilerplate. She claims we're three months behind in the rent. Is that true? Why didn't you tell me?"

"It's not your worry." Willow kissed her lightly, smiling. "I just forgot, that's all. I'll write her a check tomorrow." If she did, the check would bounce. It would have to be for twenty one hundred dollars, and there wasn't twenty one hundred dollars left. They began to climb the stairs. She said gently, "You mustn't call people Jewboy, dearest."

Mabel jerked her arm from Willow's fingers. "Oh, hell. Right away, I'm the one that shoved all six million of them into the gas ovens, right?"

"Don't be ridiculous," Willow said wearily.

"Listen, I'm happy he's a Jew," Mabel said. "It's Jews that run the picture business. Nobody else can get a foot in the door."

"That's not so. Look, I know how frustrated and angry you are and I don't blame you but it's not the fault of the Jews, Mabel. You don't like it when some redneck television preacher starts attacking the gays."

" 'Gays'!" Mabel snorted. "Dear God, what a word."

"Well, you know what I mean," Willow said.

"When's he going to read it?" Mabel reached the top of the stairs, puffing. "When's he going to call?"

"He just got back to the States," Willow said. "He has a lot to catch up on. But he promised me he'll get to it just as soon as he can."

"You mean you didn't get a bloody date from him?" Mabel sounds ready to weep. "Good God, Willow—when will you grow up? He's lying, can't you see that? He'll file it and forget it."

"You're tired," Willow said. "You need a drink and a good night's sleep."

Mabel got the drink, all right, several drinks. But no sleep—not to call sleep. She rolled from one side to the other, heavily, sweatily, all night long. She groaned. She cursed. She mumbled. Once she flung an angry arm out in some dream and her elbow bruised Willow's cheek. This was on the second night, or the third. She was a bear in the daytime. Willow went thankfully to lunch with Nash. They sat in a patio with red brick walls, white lattices, flowers everywhere.

"It's been a week," she said. "She's in an awful state."

"A week's long enough," Nash said. "Ring him up and remind him."

"I couldn't," Willow said. "He warned me he was going to be awfully busy. I believe him, Nash. He'll read it when he gets the time."

"I'll have my dad call him. They're old buddies. And you know Billy Nettles. He could make a dead mule run."

Willow sipped Perrier water and gave him a wan smile. "You shouldn't be so nice to me."

"Why not?" He regarded her gravely over a forkful of ris de veau. "You're easy to be nice to."

"I can't repay you," Willow said. "All these lovely lunches. All your comfort and advice and help."

"I care about you." He put the bite of food into his beautiful mouth and chewed. "I can't help it." He touched his beard with his napkin, sipped a little wine. "I keep hoping you'll care about me."

"I do," she said quickly, and felt her face redden. "But I can't love you, Nash. You know that." She reached to touch his hand. "I'm sorry."

"Relax." Smiling, he refilled her glass with bubbly water from a green bottle. "We're all right."

They were not all right. He ceased calling. Tuesday they ordinarily played tennis. Tuesday came and went. But he must have remembered to tell Billy Nettles to phone Gil Berger. And Billy Nettles must have done it. Because the script came back with a note. The note was crumpled in Mabel's hand when Willow, home in a rainy dusk from an AA meeting, found her clothed on the made-up bed, empty whiskey glass on the night stand, her breathing sterterous as it sometimes was when she passed out from drinking.

"Mabel?" The room was shadowy. Willow switched on the bedside lamp. The script and the brown envelope in which it had come lay on the counterpane. Mabel's fist lay on the script, clutching wadded blue paper. "Mabel?" Willow leaned over her and shook her gently by the shoulders. The slow, deep rasping of her breath went on. She did not open her eyes. But her head rolled to the side. And Willow saw a small round hole in her skull above the ear. The gray hair around the hole was singed, and blood oozed from the hole. Willow stared. She couldn't understand. Then she saw the gun in Mabel's other hand, which lay palm up, the fingers open. "Oh, my God." Willow's legs would not hold her, and she sat on the floor. She groped up for the telephone on the night stand, fumbled the receiver, caught it, and punched the button marked 0.

At eleven o'clock the next morning, she drank coffee from a paper cup in a room of the big, gaunt hospital where the glass of vending machines glared in hard, fluorescent light. Trash littered the floor, wrappers, cups, cigarette butts. The pale Formica tops of the long, steel–legged tables were sticky, stained. So were the seats of the molded plastic chairs. She had been into and out of this room a dozen times in the long night, and she had learned to wipe off any chair she wanted to sit in.

Down the hall from the emergency waiting room, this room was always in use. Even now, a speechless Mexican couple sat flanking a slim, blank-eyed, teenage boy who showed no outward signs of damage, yet appeared to Willow desperately ill. A young black woman with an arm in a new white sling sat in a corner and stared anxiously at the door to the hall, past which, in the darkest hours of the night, gurneys had hurried in a procession of wounded it seemed would never end. Above the black woman's head, rain trickled mournfully down a windowpane. The shouting and the weeping of the night, the screaming of sirens had stopped. The high white building on its hill seemed almost silent now.

Willow sipped the cardboard tasting coffee and smoked the last cigarette from a pack she'd bought in the night to give her hands something to do while she waited. Her mouth tasted terrible. Her stomach churned. She ought to eat something, anything. She pushed the chair back on its thin stuttering legs to go to the doughnut machine. And here was Nash, in a new white raincoat, damp across the shoulders, raindrops on his beautiful shoes. He was scowling, but she didn't care. She was so glad to see him, she almost burst into tears. He took her in his arms.

"Why didn't you phone me?" he said. "I had a hell of a time finding you."

"I thought we weren't speaking," she said. "Tuesday?"

"I left word with Mabel. I had to fly to New York. She didn't tell you. Jealous—right?"

"She just forgot," Willow said, against his chest.

"And you forgot I love you," Nash said.

"She's alive," Willow said, "but they don't know what to do about the bullet."

Nash looked around him at the grim room. "What did you bring her here for?"

"No money," Willow said. "You know that."

"Get her out of here, Willow." He turned toward the hall. "Can she be moved? Who's the doctor?"

"Her heartbeat is strong," Willow said. "All her vital signs. But they're afraid to touch the bullet. It's someplace dangerous. It could kill her." This did start her crying. Helplessly, she picked up the paper cup and drank from it. She put the cigarette to her mouth and drew smoke from it and blew the smoke out again, staring at him, the tears running. She bit her lip. "Ramirez," she said. "Dr. Ramirez. He looks so young."

"I'll be back," Nash said.

Willow sat on the hard little chair again. She felt grubby. Her blouse and jeans were rumpled. She was sure she smelled. She pushed at her hair. The cigarette burned her fingers, she dropped it, stepped on it. By habit she reached for the pack in her pocket and found instead the blue note, creased, crushed. In the long night, she had taken it out, opened it, and read it many times. She spread it open on the stained table top now. She didn't read the words, only stared at them. There were twenty-two. Gentle, impersonal, regretful. But Mabel had been right to avoid Gil Berger, hadn't she? Willow should never have insisted. See what she and Gil Berger had done to Mabel. Blindly, Willow folded the note again, and tucked it into her shirt pocket.

Nash came back, kissed her sweaty forehead, rubbed her back between the shoulder blades. "Go home," he said. "Get some sleep. I'll phone you when I've got her transferred."

She drove miles of rainy freeway in the Corvette, and wrestled it into the slot in the underground garage. It was more difficult than usual. She was so tired, her joints ached. She dragged up the stairs. In the patio, Parker stopped her. Rain whispered into the swimming pool, pattered on the big leaves in the corners. Parker clutched brown, wilting supermarket sacks, imprinted in red, VON'S IS GOING TO SAVE YOU. Parker's raincoat was of heavy clear plastic, silk-screened with huge hybiscus blossoms and leaves. Through a plastic hood, her hair looked like an arrangement of brass serpents. She hitched up the heavy sacks and said severely:

"Did your young man find you? My, he's persistent."

"Thank you for helping him," Willow said.

"Mabel going to be all right?" Parker said.

"I honestly don't know," Willow said.

"She drinks too much," Parker said. "Makes people feel sorry for themselves. Sure, life gets tough sometimes. I remember the Great Depression. You have to hang on. Sooner or later, things get better."

The words seemed to come from a distance. Willow's ears rang. She wasn't seeing Parker clearly. Was she going to faint? She'd never done that before. VON'S IS GOING TO SAVE YOU. She saw that plainly enough. And maybe it was going to save Parker—from what, for what, God knew. Willow didn't think it was going to save her. "I'm terribly tired," she said.

"The rent," Parker said. "Can you get that to me? It's been three months, now."

"My friend could be dying," Willow said.

"You plan to keep the apartment on your own?"

Parker hitched up the sacks again. "Where's the money coming from?"

Willow didn't have an answer. She climbed the stairs, the slim black iron railing cold under her hand, and wet with rain. In the apartment, she opened the refrigerator, and stood with the door open, eating a piece of fried chicken. And another. It was strange—Mabel not being here, not saying, "You look like hell. Where have you been all night?" Willow laid the gnawed chicken bones back on the plate, closed the refrigerator, went to the sink to wash the grease off her fingers. She did smell. She took a shower.

Seated on the closed toilet in her robe, blow-drying her hair, the little motor whining, she could see across the hall into the bedroom, where the noon light was gray with rain. The police had taken the gun away. The men in white had laid the yellow script and brown envelope on the chest of drawers before they shifted Mabel onto a gurney. The blue note had gone to the hospital clutched in Mabel's fist. Willow had brought it home. It was in the laundry hamper now, in the pocket of her shirt.

But Willow saw the bed as she had found it in the twilight yesterday, with the gun, the script, the heartless note, and bulky, drunken Mabel sunk in despair and deeper than despair. Willow switched off the dryer, hung it up, left the steamy bathroom. In the bedroom, she folded back the counterpane, pulled blankets off the bed and, stumbling with weariness, went into the lifeless livingroom, dragging the blankets behind her. Never in her life had she been so desperate for sleep. But she couldn't sleep in that bed. She slept on the couch.

The hospital to which Nash moved Mabel was on that same campus of beautiful night trees and lamplit paths where Willow used to sit listening, pleasured and at ease, to Gil Berger's rumbling voice and wry chuckle. The buildings, glass, steel, slabs of varnished wood, were so new the smell of paint still overrode the hospital smell. New or not, Willow didn't like it. The hallways were pinched. Getting down them meant dodging too many wheelchairs, too many oxygen tanks strapped to dollies, carts heaped with fresh sheets and towels, lumbering stainless steel ovens on wheels, laundry carts, orderly's mop buckets. The ceilings seemed too low. Some of their acoustic tiles had fallen already. Willow wondered how soon graffiti would appear on the walls. Yet Nash insisted that this place had the equipment and the specialists to help Mabel. If Mabel could be helped.

"But it will cost a fortune," Willow said. They were edging down one of those hallways toward elevators. They had seen Mabel. In intensive care. A starchy white hospital gown covered her. The bed was high, narrow, white, with shiny steel side bars. But she looked no different from the way she had looked on the bed at the apartment. Except for the wires and tubes attached to her. To check up on her every heartbeat, every breath. How she would hate that idea! How she would hate lying here, almost naked, for any stranger to see. Willow clasped her hands together at her chest so hard they hurt. She was willing Mabel to sit up and shout for a goddamn drink. Mabel did not. Now, at the elevator doors, Willow said, "You make me miserable. I can never pay you back, Nash."

"Your father made Billy Nettles a fortune," he said.

"Mabel never made anybody a fortune."

The elevator doors slid open. A tall man in green surgical gown and cap, mask hanging below his unshaven chin, got out. So did a middle-aged woman carrying flowers. A gurney with a pasty-faced, sedated patient on it occupied half the elevator, black orderlies standing by, looking bored. Nash and Willow got into the elevator. It stopped at every floor. When at last they got out, Nash said:

"She means everything to you." He smiled with his beautiful mouth. She couldn't see whether or not his eyes were smiling: he wore the impenetrable glasses. She thought his eyes were probably not smiling. But he said, "So that makes it the same as if it was you." He put a quick, solemn kiss on her mouth. "I'm glad it's not."

The·thought hadn't crossed her mind until he spoke, but afterward—and afterward was a long time, days and nights—she wished that since it had to be somebody, it was herself lying there in the stingy hospital gown, strung up with wires and tubes, metered, fed. She wished, instead of herself sitting here at the kitchen table drinking coffee aimless hour after hour, Mabel were sitting in the livingroom at the bar, guzzling bourbon, chain-smoking, shifting her restless weight, making the barstool creak while she fumed in anger, frustration, self-blame because Willow had tried to kill herself. Mabel had something to give the world, something fine. It was Willow's privilege to help her.

But she couldn't now. So what point was there to Willow? Another pretty face. Flowers had wilted on the kitchen table. She jerked them from the Mexican blue glass vase, threw them into the trash, and began to cry.

Boy's short yellow hair stood up as if a strong current of electricity ran through her skinny body. The black she'd smeared around her eyes made her look like a comicstrip bandit. She wore white Spandex, spike heels, a T-shirt lettered in sequinned brown-green DISGUSTING. Willow didn't know her for a minute. Nor Dorsey, either, who had packed his fatness into a tight blue 1930's thriftshop suit, and above whose frog face tilted a scruffy derby hat. Katrina, of the staring eyes and nervous, jerky chalk-white arms and legs, was the only one of the trio who looked the same as before.

When Willow saw them through the thick glass of the apartment foyer doors, she was sorry she had come down. The only human being whom she wanted to see these days was Nash, but Nash was in Washington, D. C. Only for a week. It already seemed like forever to Willow. She travelled to the hospital in the heavy Corvette twice a day, to sit beside the bed of thickly-breathing but oblivious Mabel. Otherwise she was alone. She wouldn't be less alone with Boy, Dorsey, and Katrina, and she wished they hadn't come. But they were Mabel's friends. She let them in, while Parker watched from behind hanging philodendrons, as if catching a glimpse into hell.

As Willow passed, she hissed, "I'm starting eviction proceedings against you. Tomorrow."

Willow pretended not to hear, and followed the others up the stairs. In the apartment, Boy leading, they made straight for the bar. The little refrigerator door there slapped. Ice rattled into glasses, bottles clinked. Willow stood watching, thumbnail clicking a button of her shirt. It was all right. Mabel would want them to drink. Her eyes filled with tears, imagining Mabel here at this moment, joking, bellowing laughter, waving a glass. Boy came wobbling on her spindly heels and put a cold drink into Willow's hand, who flinched and tried to give it back. "No, no," she said. "I can't. I'm alcoholic."

"We're going to drink to Mabel," Boy said, and did not take back the glass. She turned and raised her own. In a farmhouse back porch voice, she bawled, "To Mabel!"

"To a big comeback." Dorsey tipped his hat and drank.

"Poor, suffering artist." Katrina drooped tragically on a bar stool. A red kerchief banded her forehead and frizzy hair. She laid down the long, black holder into which she'd been fitting a cigarette, and lifted her glass. In her deep voice, with the Russian accent she sometimes remembered, sometimes forgot, she said, "The pain, the pain of livink." She shook her head gloomily and drank.

Willow said, "Mabel," softly, looked down into her glass, raised it, tasted the whiskey. The shock of it made her shudder. But it was a blessed shock. All these days alone, she'd shunned the bar, grimly turned her mind from it every time she'd thought of the relief a drink would bring—from sorrow, loneliness, feeling. Coffee. Coffee. Alcohol is poison to an alcoholic. It would only make things worse. God knew, they were bad enough. But now she closed her hands around the glass, and drank as if she'd been stumbling across a desert. "Mabel."

Time folded up. She was beside Boy on the couch.

"We went to see her," Boy said. "That's where we came here from—the hospital. You should have seen the looks we got. You'd think we were freaks, or something."

"You know what this is?" Dorsey stood in front of them in the awful suit, and fluttered his necktie like Oliver Hardy. "It's an old school tie. British. Veddy upper clawss. Eton. Harrow."

"It is from Exeter," Katrina moaned. "Idiot."

Dorsey glanced her way but didn't answer. He tucked the greasy tie back under his jacket. "The idea of ignorant American colonists sneering at a Dorsey—of the Dorset Dorseys. The minute you show breeding, they think you're some sort of queer."

"Not me." Boy turned on the couch, laid her head back lazily, stretched her legs across Willow's lap. It nearly made Willow spill her drink. She didn't understand why her glass was full. She kept drinking, but her glass was always full. Boy's Arkansas twang had grown twangier. "I'd never thank you was any kind of queer, Dorsey, not in a million years."

"I abhor crudity," Katrina said hollowly from the bar. "I wish at all times to be surrounded by beauty."

" 'Vissi d'arte,' " Dorsey sang in a wobbly falsetto, hand open on his chest.

"Refinement," Katrina moaned. "Taste."

"Is she going to pull out of it?" Boy asked Willow.

Willow told her about the bullet, lodged where the surgeons were afraid to go after it. "What am I going to do?" Willow felt the tears coming. "What if she never gets better? What am I going to do without her? What good am I, all by myself?"

"Don't cry." Dorsey knelt in front of her. "Here. See what I've got. This'll make you feel better."

"Dream dust?" Katrina came hurrying from the bar.

Dorsey's suit was tight, which made the pockets tight. He struggled before his plump hand came out with a clear plastic pouch. And a folder of cigarette papers.

Katrina stared. Cigarette smoke hung around her head. "Marijuana?" She sneered but she didn't walk away.

"It will cheer her up." Dorsey sat on the coffee table, unrolled the pouch, made a cigarette. Deftly. He didn't have to watch his fingers. He eyed Katrina. "You were expecting cocaine, my princess? Forget it, darling. I'm a wage slave, sweety, like you." He lit the lumpy cigarette with a limp paper match, inhaled from the cigarette, held it out to Willow, who only stared at it blankly. "It's for you, pretty gal," Boy said. "Come on, Willow. He's right. It will cheer you up." She took the cigarette from Dorsey's fingers and held it up to Willow's mouth. "Take it. Smoke it." She put it in Willow's fingers. "No good crying. Won't help Mabel none." She stroked Willow's hair. "She wouldn't want you crying. You know Mabel. She hated for anybody to cry."

It was true. Willow lifted the cigarette and drew

its harsh smoke deep into her lungs, held it, closed her eyes, let the smoke out slowly. Mabel was at her manliest, gruffest, most embarrassed, when Willow cried—which really she seldom did, seldom used to. Time folded again. Boy had one of Dorsey's handmade cigarettes, and so did Katrina, hers in the long, black holder, dribbling ash and sparks.

"Who's paying?" Dorsey coughed on smoke from his own cigarette. "Hospitals, doctors, nurses—that costs."

Willow shrugged. She was feeling better, just as they had promised.

"Insurance?" Dorsey said.

Willow laughed. "Mabel? Insurance? A worse gamble than Las Vegas, she says. Throwing money away."

"Did she sell her script?" Boy said.

"A work of genius." Katrina lay on the carpet like a bundle of bleached sticks wrapped in black, tied loosely in the middle. "Wit. Intellect. In Hollywood, who would buy such a work? The pratt-fall? The pie in the face? Where are they? How can you call this a comedy? No one gets dressed up like a gorilla. Hah!"

It was true. Willow laughed. They all laughed. Drank and smoked and laughed. And pigged in the kitchen. Everyone was ravenous. Willow, too—for the first time in many days. The kitchen was fiercely bright. Eggs broke, sour cream flowed, the can opener whined. The floor was strewn with the wrinkled tins from frozen enchiladas. Her fingers were sticky from the cinnamony syrup of a humpy-crusted apple pie—Mabel's favorite dessert. Willow had eaten her share with her fingers. So had they all.

She started for the sink. Her foot caught in an empty corn chip bag. She kicked, but the bag would not come off. She stood giving little sharp kicks and laughing, laughing till the tears ran. At last, she bent and pulled the bag off her foot and tossed it in the air. She washed her fingers at the tap, and realised she was alone in the bright kitchen. All was silent, except for the sifting of rain against the window. The window was dark. It was night outside. And in here too. That was true. It was so true, so profoundly true, that she laughed again, laughed and laughed.

Laughing, floating, she went to find the others. But the big livingroom was empty. Had they said goodnight? She couldn't remember. The lights of the city twinkled below in the rain. She found a glass at the bar and filled it with whiskey and, holding the glass, danced in the long room, whirling slowly, her feet not touching the floor, light as a feather falling, never falling, always borne up by a breeze. She knelt and fumbled, giggling, among the record albums. There it was. *La Valse*. Ms. Turntable and Mr. Pickup Arm were funny. Very gently and precisely she mated them. The music came. She sipped the whiskey, rose, and danced again, lifted by the music.

The bathroom light went on and off. Time was folded by now into a tight little packet. When a corner popped open for a moment, all was bright, sharp, perfectly clear. But when the corner fell shut again, it was dark, she was deaf, she felt nothing. She understood that she was doing the usual things she did, in the usual order. She caught glimpses of herself—the bathroom was walled along one side with mirrors. These glimpses showed her, like bright photographs in a black album, that nothing odd was happening. She was making ready for bed. As always.

A girl was in the bed, a fair, slender girl, long-limbed, with small childish breasts and slim hips. How clear her skin was, how smoothly the spare flesh lay on her young bones. This was odd. Was it herself lying in the bed? Weren't those her neat, square shoulders? But the girl turned her head now and looked at her with eyes the pale green of gooseberries. It was Boy. She had washed the black circles from her eyes and smoothed down her spiky hair. She laughed and held out her thin arms. "Come on, pretty gal," she said.

Willow looked around, bewildered. "Where's Mabel?"

"She ain't here," Boy said. "I'm here."

That was true. Willow took off her robe.

Nash said, "Willow, for God's sake, what's been going on here?" He sat on the edge of the rumpled bed and drew the stale sheet up over her. She stared at him, shivered, groped out to find the blankets but the blankets had all slipped to the floor. It was daylight, but she didn't know what day. She felt awful, moaned, turned on her face. "This apartment is like a pig sty," Nash said. "They told me at the hospital you'd come there drunk with that crazy redneck punker. They said you tried to take Mabel."

"I need a drink," Willow mumbled. She looked at him. "Please?" And when he didn't move, she called, "Boy? Get me a drink, darling. Get your pretty gal a drink?"

"She's not here." Parker said that from the bedroom doorway. "I told her if she didn't clear out, I'd call the police. Guests are one thing, but I'm not having that kind of trash moving in. Look at this place."

"Willow," Nash said, "why didn't you call AA?"

"They can't bring Mabel back." She lay turned from him, gazing at the sunny window. "They wouldn't do for me what Boy did."

"Somebody better call somebody," Parker said.

"I'll handle it, Mrs. Parker," Nash said. "It'll be all right now. You've got your check?"

"Thank you very much," Parker said stiffly. She looked around, her nose wrinkled. "You're going to need an industrial cleaning crew. I never saw anything so disgusting." She went away in her boiler-plate pants suit and brass hair. "Perverts," she said loudly, and slammed the outer door behind her.

Willow turned and looked at Nash through tears. "Oh, Nash, why were you gone so long?"

He gathered her in his arms. "I'm back, now," he said. "You'll be all right, now."

But she was not all right. She had starved her body, the alcohol had ravaged it, and her mind was sick. It was weeks before she could leave the place to which he had taken her, a sprawl of new, low-roofed, quiet buildings among hills in the west valley. There was television, but it tired her to watch it. From the windows of her pleasant room—she was a prisoner, but they did their best to make it seem not so—she could gaze out at oaks on the hills, white-faced cattle grazing, sometimes horses. When her strength began to return and they let her go outside for an hour a day, she could smell the sea on the wind. She watched the clouds as if she were a child.

Nash came to see her as often as he could, bringing flowers, books, magazines. And, when he judged Willow was able to hear it, word of Mabel. She lay in a coma. She had lost weight but her heartbeat was strong, her lungs were clear, her kidneys and other organs went on functioning as if nothing were wrong. A specialist from Boston had come and gone. He could see no way of removing the bullet without killing the patient.

"How long can it go on?" Willow said.

"I asked him that," Nash said. "Maybe for years."

She turned her face away. "Poor Mabel."

He touched her. "Poor Willow," he said.

On the clear, warm, breezy morning when Nash came to fetch her away, her jeans and shirts in a leather tote bag, books in a string-tied bundle, and a goodbye bouquet from some fellow patients, he did not drive south and inland toward the city, but north and west instead, toward the sea. At Ventura, they rode horses by the sea. The blue waves sparkled in the sun. The fresh wind fluttered her hair and the dark manes and tails of the horses. The hoofs of the horses crunched sand swept clean by a tide that slipped whispering toward them and slipped back out again. Willow felt frail but happy. She stroked the strong, bending neck of her horse, sleek and alive beneath her hand. She turned to smile at Nash. His back was to her. He was looking down, tugging at a stirrup strap. His neck was bent as her horse's was, strong, sleek, and alive.

The apartment was not simply clean and orderly again. It was redecorated. It was as it had been the day when she and Mabel moved into it. But of course, Mabel was not here, so though it was beautiful, it was desolate. All trace of Mabel had vanished, Mabel, who had meant to leave a mark on the world, to be remembered everywhere forever. And here, at the center of her life, love, work, hope, there remained not so much as a twisted cigarette butt or an empty beer can to say, Mabel was here. Mournfully, Willow rolled back the doors of the bedroom closet. There, among shoes on the floor, sat the stack of scripts and Mabel's typewriter, put out of the way by the painters. And here hung Mabel's clothes—the wide jeans for her bulky hips, the lumberjack shirts, the leather jackets. Willow hid her face in them and wept.

"It is too bad," Emil Pollock said. "Tragic." He sat wrapped in his soiled kitchen apron at one of the little red-checked tables in the Hungry Hungarian. Lunch was over, dinner was a long time off, and the place was empty and still. The big fat man said, "I hate to think of her so sad. I loved to hear her laugh." His face was red, sweat glistened on his bald dome, and his childlike blue eyes looked tenderly at Willow. "But I don't know what to say to you, dear little Willow. It is hard work, being a waitress. On your feet all the time, run, run—never a moment's rest."

"I have strong legs," Willow said, "and good endurance. I know I don't look it, but I'm strong. I play tennis all the time."

Emil's sweaty forehead rumpled. "But this is just a small, little place." He gestured, dropped his hands to the table cloth again. His fingers were like sausages. He interlaced them, as if in prayer. "I can pay only minimum wage, you know? It isn't a decent living. Not what you are used to, nothing like that."

"There'd be tips," Willow said.

Emil grunted a brief laugh. "Of course. But you never know." His shoulders bulged like beef roasts under the white fabric of his shirt. He raised and lowered them. "People are not always generous. Sometimes, if something doesn't suit them, the food is not the way they want, the wine, the woman— they leave no tip at all."

"I've been trying," Willow said bleakly, feeling tears want to start. "I can't get an office job. You have to know typing and computers and I don't. Please, Emil. I'll be helpful to you, I promise. I can cook a little, you know. Wash dishes, mop floors."

"Poor little Willow." He sighed, patted her hand on the table, and heaved to his feet. "All right." He nodded with a small, sad smile. "We try. We see. Okay? You come today, four thirty."

"Willow, for God's sake, what does this mean?" It was Nash, standing in the dim brown hall that smelled of dried peppers and masa and chile powder from the Mexican grocery downstairs. "I'm gone for one miserable month, and look at you."

He took off his opaque glasses and frowned past her into the tiny apartment. He was back from London, Brussels, Paris. "I don't understand you. Why?"

"Come in." She yawned, pushed at her uncombed hair, smiled sleepily. "I'm glad to see you." He'd wakened her. The apartment didn't have even a window air conditioner, the nights were hot, she'd slept naked, and pulled on the nearest tanktop and jeans her hand came to. They were soiled and rumpled. She was sorry. His cool grooming shamed her. "Excuse how I look. I didn't expect you. I guess I thought you'd gone for good this time."

"I'm going to have to give up traveling." He stood in the room, looking at the tumbled, sweaty sheets on the convertible sofa, the thin blanket fallen to the floor. "You do crazy things on your own."

For an instant, she saw the place through his eyes—the nicked Mexican-pink chest of drawers, the cheap frameless mirror over the chest, the two ravelled wicker barrel chairs at a formica-topped table with spindly steel legs, the lamps with discolored shades, her books and records stacked on the floor, the floor itself, pale vinyl tile no one had waxed in years. Well, he didn't have to like it. Nor did she. It was simply a place to shelter in, sleep in.

"This was a smart thing," she said, "not a crazy thing. I'm fine here." Next to a mayonnaise jar that held fresh flowers on the table stood a cheap new little radio. "See? I can even have music when I want it. Sit down." She gave him a little kiss. "And stop looking grim." She went to an alcove that held smudged cupboards, a sink, a trembly little refrigerator, a hotplate. "I'll make some coffee." She filled a kettle, set it on a burner. "What time is it? Isn't it awfully early?"

"You're working nights at some grubby hash house."

"And days," she said, "but it's not a grubby hash house. It's a very nice little Hungarian restaurant with wonderful food. I'll take you there on my night off. You'll see." She laid a filter in the basket of a dented aluminum pot, spooned in coffee, an extra scoop so he wouldn't notice it was a cheap brand. "You mustn't believe what Parker says."

"That was a beautiful apartment," he said. "This is a rat hole, Willow. The neighborhood! You'll be raped and murdered down here."

"You sound like Mabel." A trailing plant in a brown plastic pot hung by the narrow kitchen window. She touched the soil in the pot, filled a drinking glass, watered the plant. "Why is it everyone who loves me thinks I'm going to be raped and murdered? It's very quiet, actually. And the Esperanzas downstairs are very nice. The couple who own the grocery store. They think I'm a poor little rich girl. They keep an eye on me."

"There's graffiti everywhere," Nash said. "That means street gangs, Willow. And street gangs are no joke." He lit a cigarette. The smoke smelled strange to Willow. The pack lay on the table. It was blue. He had brought home Gauloises. "Don't tell me," he said, "that they haven't stripped your car, yet."

"I don't leave it on the street." She went and sat at the table and touched the cigarette pack. "May I?"

"Help yourself," he said, "but they're strong."

"Mabel loved them," Willow said. But when Nash lighted one for her, she coughed. "Whew!" She laughed. Through the curling smoke, she said soberly, "The rent at Parker's was seven hundred dollars a month. You know that. You were paying it. And that wasn't right." She glanced around the sorry room. "This only costs a hundred fifty."

"And worth every penny," he said.

"At least I can afford it," she said. "And see here." She got out of the crackly chair and hurried to the kitchenette. She crouched at a lower cupboard, reached into the back, brought out a coffee can. She set this on the table, sat down, peeled the plastic lid off the can, and brought out a wad of paper money. "I've been able to put all this aside. They like me at the Hungry Hungarian. They leave me lovely tips." Nash frowned at the crumpled bills. She pushed them toward him. "For you. The first instalment on what I owe you. It's not much, but it's a start." Nash put his hands behind him, around the low back of the chair. Willow cried, "What's the matter? It's for the rent at Parkers, for Mabel's hospital bills, my hospital bills. I know it must come to thousands and thousands, but I'll pay it all back. I'm working hard, Nash. Honest."

"Oh, Willow." He shook his head in despair. He gathered up the money, stuffed it back into the coffee can, and clapped the lid on. He took the can back into the kitchenette. Squatting, he thrust the can back into its cupboard, and closed the cupboard door, which was crooked, and swung half open again right away.

"What are you doing?" Willow ran to him. "It's

yours. You have to take it. I've been saving it for you." She tried to push him away from the cupboard so she could get the can out again. He stood up. "It's not fair, Nash." She beat at him with fists that seemed to her small and childlike. He caught her wrists. She struggled. "Don't. Let me go. You have to let me try, Nash. You have to."

"Willow, stop. Calm down." He waited, and she gave a sharp sigh and relaxed. He closed her in his arms, kissed her ear, whispered a sad laugh. "You don't understand. Billy Nettles collects tremendous commissions and legal fees all the time." The kettle on the hotplate began to whistle. He reached past her and turned the burner down. "Those get invested, right? And the investments pay interest and dividends. Money making more money, see?" He peered into her eyes, smiled, let her go, picked up the kettle and poured water from it into the coffeepot. "I get a share of all of it. Over and above what I get paid, which is ridicuous in itself." He set the kettle back on the hot plate. The water made a drizzling sound in the thin, tinny pot. The steam that rose from it smelled good. Nash led Willow back to the table and set her down. "Now, what we're going to do is have a nice cup of coffee and a cigarette, and you're going to listen to me— with your mind, not your emotions, okay?" She looked up at him meekly. He gave his head a grim little shake and went back to pour the coffee. He called, "You work too hard to give your money away."

"You work hard," she said. "Day and night."

"But you earn your money," he said. "I don't. No one 'earns' a hundred thousand dollars a year." He set dimestore mugs of coffee on the table, and sat down. "And that doesn't include the extras that pour into bank accounts I don't even keep track of. And that's earning interest, too, isn't it?" He laughed helplessly. "Don't you see, dear, innocent Willow—that kind of money isn't even real."

"All kinds are real to me." She went to the window. Behind the building next door, a slim Mexican boy sat on a kitchen chair, practicing his guitar. Raoul. He sometimes helped in the store. He always smiled at her. Small brown brothers and sisters romped around him. Willow said, "It seemed so kind. Now you say it didn't mean anything."

"I say it didn't cost anything. That's different. I meant it to be kind." A break in his voice made her turn and look at him. He said, "I love you, Willow. That's why I did it. I could do it, and I was damned thankful I could do it, and I want you to allow me to go on doing it, okay? You mustn't try to pay me back. Don't you see—money's all you ever let me give you."

"And all I give you is pain." She twisted out the cigarette, set down her mug, and left the table. She jerked the sheets straight on the bed, snatched up the blanket, flapped it over the bed, tucked in the corners. "Nash, I'm not going to change. I can't." Her teeth were clenched so hard they hurt. She folded the bed shut, and blinded by tears, picked up the stacked cushions from the floor and laid them on the couch. She faced him, fists tight, the room a wet blur. "If I could dream of having sex with any man, it would be you. But that isn't how I dream. It isn't how I am. And that"—she shook her head angrily to keep from crying—"is why you must, must, must let me pay you back."

He watched her for a long moment, motionless,

with sorrow in his soft brown eyes. His smooth skin
and trim little beard made him look like a painting. He sighed, put out his cigarette, got to his feet.
The impenetrable glasses lay on the table. He
picked them up and put them on. "You use that
money to rent yourself a decent apartment." He
walked to the door. "I'll worry till you get out of
here."

"They sell money orders down in the grocery
store," she said. "Every week, I'm going to send you
a hundred dollars, Nash. Every week, no matter
how long it takes."

He stood at the door, aimlessly twisting the bolt
in and out, watching his fingers, his back to her.
"Your rockabilly friend. Does she come around?
Boy? Was that what she called herself?"

"No one comes around. Mabel's the only one I
see." Willow went to him, reached past him, pulled
open the door. "Don't come back, Nash." She put
a quick, solemn kiss on his mouth. "Forget me."

Nash took off the glasses. "If you want to pay
me back, marry me. You'll have all that money from
your father's estate. I don't want the money. I want
you. You're all I want. But you want to pay me
back—so marry me, Willow. You don't have to sleep
with me. But you'll be living decently. You won't
have to wait on tables."

Willow smiled. "If I don't sleep with you, where
am I going to get a baby from? And if I don't have
a baby, I don't get my father's money, remember?"

He shrugged. "So, we'll make a baby. It's not
complicated. People do it every day." He gave her
a wistful smile. "Who knows? You might even de-
cide you like it."

She shut her eyes, rested her forehead on the door frame. Below, in the yard next door, Raoul stopped playing exercises and began a tune. It took her back to Mazatlan. With Mabel. That was fun. She sighed, opened her eyes. "I'll think about it," she said. "Thank you."

"You will?" He was surprised, excited, pleased.

"Not really." She had bought a woven straw donkey in Mazatlan. What had become of it? She told Nash, "I just don't know what to say to you." She raised her hands and let them drop helplessly. "I don't know how to handle this." Tears were starting again. She blinked them back. "Just go, Nash—all right?"

"You're punishing yourself for nothing," he said.

"I'm just working, eating, sleeping," she said, "like ordinary people, trying not to do anybody any harm. I hate hurting you all the time and I can't help it. That's why I say go and don't come back."

"Whatever you say." He put on the glasses, started down the brown hallway. A cat licked milk from a saucer outside an apartment door. He crouched to pet the cat. It was black and white, young and thin. It arched its back under Nash's hand, lifted its head, eyes half-closed in ecstasy, and purred. Nash said, "But I won't stop worrying about you." He scratched the cat's ears.

"Worry about yourself," she said. "Find a woman who will make you happy."

"I already have." Nash left off petting the cat and stood. The cat rubbed against his pantleg. He smiled down at it ruefully. "See how simple love can be?"

Willow closed her door.

Billy Nettles had not changed, but she hardly knew him at first, it was so long since she'd seen him. He came into the Hungry Hungarian, gaunt and gangly, in rumpled seersucker, limp shirtcollar, a string tie, and hung a Panama on the coat rack by the door. Marta, big Emil's tiny sister, met him. He bent over her like a wading bird over a cricket, spoke, and she led him to the only one of Willow's tables not occupied, in a far corner where heat from the kitchen reached. Marta had once been a ballerina. She still moved, at sixty, as if an orchestra were playing inside her head—scarcely seeming to touch the floor. Billy sat down, she put a menu into his knuckly hands, and floated over to Willow.

"He is a stranger," she whispered, "but he asked for you." She glanced worriedly over her shoulder at Billy. "Is it all right? Felina can take that table."

"It's all right." Willow mixed tarragon vinegar with olive oil from a gold half gallon tin. Salads, lettuce, tomato, cucumber, lay on plates in front of her. She poured on the dressing, sprinkled the salads with pepper from a wooden mill. "He's an old family friend. I haven't seen him in years."

"Ah! A reunion!" Marta's dark eyes shone. She put her hands flat together at her sharp little chin, and smiled. "Shall I open champagne? Yes, yes." She started to hurry away.

"No, please. It won't be a celebration."

"Not?" Marta turned back, surprised, disappointed. "Something unpleasant?"

Willow gathered up the chill salad plates, gave Marta a smile and a shake of her head. "Just business, I imagine," she said, and whisked away.

When she went to Billy's table, he got up lankily and shook her hand, but it was forty minutes before the demands of the diners at the other tables slacked off enough so that she could sit down with him and hear why he'd come. The fork looked awkward in his big, gnarled hand as he finished off his turkey goulash. Emil served very large helpings, but Billy had eaten his and a basket of bread besides. How did he do it and stay so thin? Willow's mother used to ask him that at every meal she served him. Willow could hear her voice now, asking him. He laid the fork down and mopped his plate with all that remained of his bread, the heel. He poked the gravy-soaked thing into his mouth and chewed, his big ears moving. He washed the mouthful down with a long drink of beer. His Adam's apple moved up and down in his long, stringy throat. This used to fascinate Willow when she was small. He sighed, wiped his mouth with his napkin, laid the napkin beside his plate, sat back in his chair and, while he unwrapped a cigar, looked at Willow. His face was long, furrowed, mournful, but there was always a smile behind his eyes. It was there now. He lit the cigar with a kitchen match, shook out the match, reached to drop it in the ashtray by the candle in its amber chimney, and said:

"You know, your daddy can't see you here. No way can you make him even a little bit mad being a waitress, running your legs off, getting blisters on your feet. He don't know, and he don't care. Not anymore."

"I'll get you coffee." Willow started to rise.

Billy held up a hand. "In a minute. Just answer my question, first, please. What are you trying to prove, and who are you trying to prove it to?"

"Nothing." She got up. "No one." She went for

the coffee urn, came back and filled his cup, went to her other tables to fill cups there. She put the urn back and returned to him. "Oh, maybe something. To myself." She sat down. "Only myself, Billy."

He watched her with those gently laughing eyes for a moment, then busied himself putting sugar and cream into his coffee. He made quite a rattling with the spoon in the cup, and a clatter laying the spoon in the saucer. "If it was within your nature," he said, lifting the cup, tasting the coffee, "you'd have taken up streetwalking to shame him, give him fits. Now, isn't that true?"

"You said yourself, he doesn't know and doesn't care."

"I said it." Billy's big, sad head nodded. His shock of white hair moved thickly. "You didn't. You're still pretty much a girl child yet. It takes some of us a long time to get out from under our folks. Some of us never do—parents can be dead and gone for years, for a lifetime, but we're still proving something to them, generally that they were all wrong about us."

"He was wrong," Willow said sharply. "I didn't suit his idea of what his little girl should be. And what was his answer? To love me as I was? No. To change me, to force me to change. To bribe me to change. It was all he understood. Anything he wanted could be bought. And when his little girl showed him that wasn't so—then he took away his money."

"Some of us," Billy Nettles said, "can be pretty exacting when it comes to other people's shortcomings."

"Being a lesbian is not a shortcoming," Willow said.

"Sorry. Misspoke myself. I stand corrected."

"I didn't want his money," Willow said, "not on his terms. I can get along just fine"—her voice trembled with anger—"just fine, without him. He's still trying to bribe me to be his creature instead of myself. From the grave, Billy."

"We-e-ll." Billy blew a long trail of cigar smoke into the air. "The thing that's wrong here is—he's reaching you, but you're not reaching him. One-sided situation." He studied her. "Nash loves you, you know."

"And you're telling me that because my father is dead and won't get any satisfaction from it, I should marry Nash, and have a child, and collect two hundred fifty thousand dollars—right?" She watched Billy turn his cigar in the little ashtray. "Well, it isn't going to happen. It would only mean misery for both of us. Surely you can see that."

"I don't see two very happy youngsters, right now, the way things stand." His wide mouth twitched a regretful smile. "Looks to me as if you're about as stiff-necked as your old man. Like father, like daughter."

Somewhere in Willow's mind, Nash said, *You know Billy Nettles—he could make a dead mule run.* She said to Billy, "Did Nash send you here? To plead his cause? Surely not. That's two against one. Nash wouldn't do that."

"Nope, he wouldn't." Billy drank some more coffee, rattled the cup back into the saucer. "And he didn't. Nor is that the reason I came here on my own. I came because you're working too hard here. This kind of work doesn't pay decent wages. You come join my staff. I'll put you to work looking up references in the law library. You can learn the job in a day. Nothing to it."

Willow shook her head. "I'd be seeing Nash."

"No need. Not if you didn't want to. It pays four fifty a week, and you won't be running yourself ragged. It's sit-down work."

She stood up. "I have tables to clear."

"I'll go." Billy unfolded his bony length and looked gravely down at her. "You think about it. If you want to pay Nash back for those hospital bills your friend's running up, you owe it to her to make the most wages you can." He tucked a ten dollar bill under his saucer, gave her a clumsy pat, and shambled away between the empty tables to pay Marta for his meal. Then he took down his hat from the rack, and went out into the twilight.

Willow sat by Mabel's hospital bed and stared wanly at wallpaper printed with big, cheerful, yolk yellow nasturtiums. Outside the open door, medication carts jingled along the corridor, the crepe soles of nurses' shoes squeaked, electronic chimes pinged, telephones burred softly. Wired to monitors, fed and drained by tubes, Mabel lay motionless, silent except for soft, regular snores. Willow understood that they turned her this way and that, to prevent bedsores. But she always lay on her back when Willow saw her. She was dreadfully thin, now. It pained Willow to look at her. But she talked to her. Who else was there to talk to?

"You just know that kind of job doesn't pay any

four fifty a week." She laughed scornfully. "I'll bet it doesn't pay two hundred. To look up references in a library? No way. It's charity. And trying to pull me into the firm, into the family, into Nash's bed."

"Are you all right?" A young woman stood in the doorway, ruddy, brown-eyed, dark hair cut short. For a moment, Willow didn't recognize her. Where was her intern's white coat with the I. D. badge pinned to it? Now she wore a fringed leather jacket, corduroy skirt, fringed leather boots. "She can't hear you, you know."

"Does anyone know? Do you know, doctor?"

"She doesn't answer, does she?"

Willow shook her head, sighed, stood up, feeling the ache in her legs that never seemed to leave them anymore—waiting tables was nothing like tennis. Barred sides were raised on Mabel's bed. Science was wonderful: someone thought she might suddenly move. Willow wished it was true. She reached down and held Mabel's limp hand for a moment. It was neither warm nor cool—room temperature, rather, like a piece of furniture. Willow said, gazing at the beloved face, so changed, "Maybe I shouldn't talk to her. Maybe I disturb her dreams. Maybe she's having pleasant dreams."

"Is she your mother?"

"What a thought," Willow said. "No, she's no one's mother. The idea of motherhood appalled her."

"What about a cup of coffee?" The doctor—Willow remembered the name typed on the celluloid covered card now: Dr. Ellen McMahon—ventured a smile. "If you talk to me, at least I can answer. I can try."

"I only have one day off a week," Willow said, "to shop and get my hair cut, clean house, do the laundry. That's ahead of me tonight—the laundromat." She returned Ellen McMahon's smile. "Maybe next time."

"I'll look forward to it."

Willow stripped her bed, stuffed sheets and pillowcases into a big green plastic trash bag, along with underwear and socks, shirts and jeans. The look in the doctor's eyes stayed with her. She shrugged it off. She didn't want Ellen McMahon. She wanted Mabel. Blinking back tears, she dragged the bag to the door, opened the door, set the spring lock. She swung the bag into the hallway, pulled the door shut behind her, and bumped the bag after her down the stairs. It was heavy. She'd let too much wash accumulate—too tired on her days off to face chores.

A faint light burned inside the grocery store, behind the cash register at the checkout counter. Folding steel grills were pulled across the window and door, and padlocked. The store had often been robbed. Now it was never open at night. Willow saw movement inside, and her heart skipped a beat. But it was only Senor Esperanza, stocky, gray-haired. He saw Willow, scowled, shook his head, and waved an urgent arm to motion her back the way she had come. Willow stared. He hurried to the door, a rifle in his hand. He mouthed through the thick plate glass of the door:

"Stay home tonight. There will be trouble."

"Don't worry," she called, her voice echoing

cheery and childlike down the empty street, "I'll be all right."

She gave him a smile and a wave and, clutching the bulky bag to her, headed toward the brightly-lighted little shopping center at the far corner. The sidewalks were deserted. No one sat on doorsteps, talking. Always children ran up and down, calling out, playing. Not tonight. No young men clustered around the lifted hoods of old cars, drinking beer, pondering the cars' ailments. The only traffic on the street moved slowly. The cars gleamed with metallic paint in ferocious purples and greens, rear ends sunk low or boosted high on big, broad tires with raised white lettering. Inside the cars sat youths with smooth brown faces, luminous brown eyes. Some scowled. Others grinned, but not cheerfully. Like Senor Esperanza, Mabel and Nash would be horrified to know that Willow was out here tonight. But Willow wasn't worried. The boys were a threat to each other, not to her.

The glass doors of the bright laundromat stood open. Willow lugged the heavy bag inside where rows of sleek washers vibrated, where colored clothes tumbled behind round glass in the doors of driers. Korean women, middle-aged, old, arranged fresh shirts on hangers or between them folded unmatched patterned sheets bought at sales. A heavy-breasted black woman loaded a washer from a bright yellow plastic basket. This was mainly a chicano neighborhood. Where were the Spanish-speaking women tonight?

The change machine by the windows swallowed her dollar bills and gave her back quarters. She bought from another coin machine small boxes of detergent and bleach. Tires squealed on paving. It was a sudden sound, loud in the neighborhood quiet. Willow glanced at the street, but saw only a group of boys in shiny jackets gathered at a taco stand across the way. She filled three washers from her plastic bag, laid quarters in the coin feeds, set the dials, closed down the lids, pushed in the coins. Two of the Korean women—a mother and daughter, Willow thought—went out and loaded folded laundry into a Japanese hatchback. While Willow bought a coke from a machine in a front corner of the place, they drove away.

Willow sat on a pink moulded plastic chair beside the coke machine. The black woman waddled to a chair in a row with its backs against the window, sat down, placed a shopping bag beside her, pulled newspapers from the shopping bag. Also a pair of scissors. She began to leaf through the newspapers and cut out food coupons. The youngest of the Korean women took her laundry and her little car away. Someplace out in the dark, tires gave protracted screams again, and engines roared. Maybe the gang boys were racing. Willow hoped so. If they were racing, they weren't fighting, trying to kill one another. The oldest Korean woman, very small and withered, had put her finished laundry into a little wire cart she wheeled behind her. She hobbled away on foot, in jogging shoes.

The hum of the washers, the methodical rattle of the newspaper pages, the sibillance of the black woman's scissors were for a time the only sounds. She took a paperback book from her hip pocket. If she didn't read, she would keep looking at the clock, and there was no point in that. Tires screamed again, not far off this time. Engines roared and rumbled. The street began to fill with the gaudy cars, lurching, rocking on their springs, halting at odd angles. The black woman stood up to look. Raoul appeared, panting, in the doorway, glancing around, worried. By the Coke machine, Willow was out of his line of sight. She got off the chair, he saw her. He smiled but his eyes were anxious.

"Are you all right?"

Shouts came from the street. Car doors slammed.

Willow said, "Did Senor Esperanza send you?"

"The gangs are going to fight. He wants me to bring you home." Raoul wore a shirt too big for him, probably his father's. It made him look about twelve years old. He glanced at the street through the wide, high windows. "We better go out the back way."

"Sit down." She hadn't touched her coke. She handed it to him. "This is the only night I have to do my wash."

"No." He reached past her to set the bottle on the machine. He took her arm. "Come. Please. Hurry."

"My clothes." She opened a washer. Dirty suds. "I can't just go leave my clothes."

"This place is open all night." He ran for the back door. The shouting in the street grew angrier. Raoul said, "We can get your clothes later. Come on." He pulled at the door. The black woman snatched up her shopping bag.

"They going to fight right here," she said.

Willow let the lid of the washer drop. Sirens

wailed. The black woman hurried toward Raoul, her massive buttocks rolling. Willow called, "It's all right. The police are coming. Hear the sirens?"

"It not all right with me." The black woman flapped the shopping bag into her yellow plastic basket. "They got guns. You look out there, see for yourself." She pushed at Raoul. "Open that door. Open it. Open it."

"It is locked," he said. He tugged frantically at the knob. "How can they do that?" He gave the door a kick and turned back. "How? How can they lock the door?"

Guns went off in the street. The noise was loud and flat. Behind her, Willow heard the plate glass of the laundromat shatter and crash down in sections. She did not turn to look. She stared at Raoul. He was trying to speak to her. A bloodstain flowered on the white cloth of the shirt that was too big for him. He fell back against the door. He put a hand on the bloodstain, slumped to his knees, toppled forward on his face. The black woman dropped the yellow basket and clapped her hands to her fat cheeks.

"Oh, my Lord," she said. "Oh, my Jesus."

The siren wails grew loud. More tires squealed. The shooting stopped. A pay telephone was sheltered by a blue plastic bubble outside the laundromat. Willow ran across broken plateglass and out the door. On the street, black and white patrol cars boxed in the garish cars of the gang boys. Rifle barrels swung high in the hands of police officers. The crash helmets of the officers gleamed as if wet, in the cold greenish glare of the streetlights. The gang boys lay face down on the pavement. Willow took down the receiver and dropped a dime into the pay phone. She pushed the 0 button. At the other end of the line, a telephone rang and rang. A police officer, middle-aged, paunchy, smelling of leather, came to her. He wore wrap-around dark glasses, and his crash helmet was scratched.

"Excuse me, miss," he said, "did you see anything?"

"There's a boy in there." She waved her free hand. Her voice was shrill. "He's shot. I'm phoning for an ambulance."

"Save your dime." The officer's black gloved hand took the receiver from her and hung it up. "An ambulance is on its way." He turned away. "Show me where he is."

She showed him. He knelt with a grunt and touched Raoul, who lay very still. Willow said, "You're not supposed to move injured people."

"I know that," he said. "He's breathing. There's a heartbeat. Losing a lot of blood, here." He got heavily to his feet. "How did it happen—do you know?"

She told him. She told a detective in blue jeans when he came. By that time, ambulance people were wheeling Raoul away on a gurney. An attendant held at arm's height a plastic sack of plasma attached by a tube to Raoul's thin arm. As the gurney passed her, bumping on the broken glass, he opened his eyes and gave her a fragile smile. "Ah, you are okay," he said, and closed his eyes again. With hard jarring sounds, the legs of the gurney folded at the open ambulance doors. The man with the plasma climbed up inside as the gurney slid in. The other attendant slammed the rear doors and ran to climb into the cab, and the ambulance tilted out the driveway into the street, its siren starting to moan.

"Where are they taking him?" Willow said.

The detective said, "County Medical Center."

The black woman opened the washroom door a crack. It had a coin lock. She peered out. "Is it over?"

The detective flipped open his wallet to show her a badge. "Ma'am? Did you see what happened?"

She came out of the washroom, shaken, solemn. The front of her red and white striped cotton blouse was water-soaked. "I was standing right next to him. Got his blood on me. Been trying to wash it off."

They were a long time at the laundromat. The detective in the blue jeans seemed uncertain. He kept telling Willow and the black woman, whose name was Mrs. Morris, to wait, and wandering outside to where the excitement was, in the street, police radios giving off loud, harsh bursts of talk, cars and men arriving and leaving. The detective kept bringing back with him different plainclothes officers, but none of them knew quite what to do with Willow and Mrs. Morris. The women's names, addresses, and statements were in several notebooks. At last, the detective in blue jeans told them they were free to leave. Mrs. Morris grumpily pulled her wet wash out of the machines and dumped it into driers. Willow looked into her washers at her clothes, plastered miserably against the dark blue rounded insides, and didn't know what to do, and left everything.

At the County Medical Center, she lost her way,

trying to find where they had put Raoul. The lights seemed very bright, and all the clean corridors alike, with their carts and night-shift nurses, doctors, orderlies, nameless, featureless. She rode elevators up, got lost, rode elevators down. She asked directions, and got lost again. It was like a dream. She gave up in an empty corridor, sat down on the shiny floor, her back against the cold wall, and for a time must have slept. When she awoke, she couldn't think why she was here. She got up wearily and went looking again for the signs she had been told to look for. She was exhausted, that was all. Of course, she knew why she was here. Then she found the place she had been looking for. And someone else asked her the question.

"Why are you here?" It was gnarled Ruben Martinez, brown leathery skin, cheeks sunken and pockmarked. "You are the cause of this." He glared at her. Tears lay in the creases of his face. "You are the reason my boy is in there, dying."

"A young boy—all his life before him." This was Anna Maria, Raoul's mother, plump, with large, soft eyes. "He was too young for you." She sniffled, and held a wadded handkerchief to her blunt nose. "What kind of person are you, to lead a young boy to his death?"

Bewildered, appalled, Willow shook her head. "Senor Esperanza sent him."

"You know nothing," Ruben Martinez said. "Raoul saw you going down the street. From our window. He asked to go and warn you of the danger. I forbid it. I am his father. What judgment does he have?"

"We kept him from those gangs," Anna Maria

said. "We are not that kind. We kept him in his home where he belongs. And now look. Now look what has happened."

"He told us he was going to bed," Martinez said, "but instead he went to save you."

"But it wasn't my fault." Willow held her hands out, tears in her eyes.

"It is your fault," Martinez said, "for being where you do not belong. A rich girl, spoiled. The grocer told me. What is someone like you doing living among us?"

"Turning the heads of young boys," Anna Maria said.

Willow looked down at herself. Yes, the bulky sweater had cost a lot. But that was long ago, in another life. It was ravelled and shapeless now. The very expensive jeans, too—worn, faded. "I work," she said. "Like you. You see me go to work. Every day."

"You need a husband," Martinez said. "You do not know how to look after yourself. This is not Beverly Hills. You put yourself in foolish danger. And for that, a young boy dies."

"Maybe not," Willow said. "Maybe they'll save him."

Martinez shook his head. "No. He has the blood of the old Spanish kings." His wife turned away, weeping. Willow did not understand the man, and her face must have showed it. "Hemophelia" he said. "The blood will not stop flowing from the wound."

The baby kicked sometimes in her swollen belly, very sharply. It was supposed to be amusing, but it hurt. Did all that vigor mean, as the doctor said, that it was healthy, or that it was like Willow herself, in a place it did not want to be, kicking silently to get out? Well, at least it had the darkness. This house, with its great windows gaping on the sea, and its high, white rooms, punished her with brightness all day long. There was no escaping it.

At first, she wasn't here all the time. Nash took her with him on his trips. True, the villa in Genoa had glared like this, but Paris had only the pewter mirror of the Seine to reflect the temperate sun, and scruffy old London had no sun at all, just rain and gloom. She longed for London now. But the doctor did not want her traveling, and she herself dreaded sitting in cramped aircraft seats for ten, twelve hours at a stretch. Restless as the baby inside her, she needed to move around. She missed tennis. A short morning jog along the beach was all she was permitted, and jogging was a lonely business that left her free to think. And all her thoughts were bleak. Indoors, the persistent sunlight only made them bleaker, the rooms emptier, more alien.

She gave her head a shake, and reached across the guitar on her knees—almost off her knees, these days, the baby bulged so—to flip back the page of a music book on a couch cushion beside her. Even the fabric on the furniture was white. She frowned at the guitar chord diagrams above the staves where notes scampered gaily on, defying her to catch and identify them. She was not musical, and the guitar strings hurt her fingertips. But trying to learn kept her from thinking, and made the time pass. The baby kicked again. She winced. And the telephone rang.

It didn't ring—it gave an electronic cry. But in the long room with its hard surfaces of plaster and glass, it was loud. She laid the guitar on the music book and went barefoot along the cool tiles to the white couch, chairs, lamps on low tables grouped facing the blue ocean and a long blue curve of shoreline. The sun struck hot through the glass here. The tile-red telephone instrument was warm in her hand. She stood in the arched-back stance that carrying unborn young imposed on woman-kind and felt an ache in her lower spine. She said into the telephone, "Willow Nettles," and smiled to herself at how botanical a creature marriage had made her sound. She spoke her name because it was the wrong hour for Nash to be calling. She couldn't think who would call her other than Nash. He was in Hong Kong.

"This is University Hospital. Miss Talbot? In administrations?"

Willow's knees gave. She sat down. "No," she said.

"We have instructions to contact you," the voice went on heedlessly, "in regard to the condition of a patient—Mabel Stoner?"

"Yes—I'm her guardian," Willow said faintly. Billy Nettles had arranged that. It had some legal meaning, but Willow thought it was a strange, cold word for what she was to Mabel. It made Mabel her ward, which was stranger still, and colder. "What's happened? She's dead, isn't she?" Willow heard her voice, thin, high, trembly, echoing off the window glass. Grief was rising to drown her. She fought it back. "Well, listen to me," she shouted into the telephone. "I'm pregnant. I'm going to have a baby. And I'm going to name her Mabel, understand? I don't care whether Nash hates it or not."

The telephone line hissed quietly for a few seconds. Then Miss Talbot said, "Miss Stoner isn't dead, Mrs. Nettles. She's regained consciousness. She's asking to see you."

"You took your time getting here," Mabel said. She was in a different room, on a different floor. The curtains were drawn. It was dim, but the white of bandages showed, a sling, her arm was in a sling. "The clumsy sons of bitches damn near killed me."

"Mabel, what are you talking about?"

"They didn't tell you, did they?" Mabel tried to hitch herself higher in the bed. "They dropped me, stupid niggers. Lifting me to change the bed. Dropped me on the floor. Broke my shoulder."

Willow's knees gave again. She took the small moulded plastic chair beside the bed. "It was an accident."

"It was an accident they're going to remember," Mabel said. "You better believe it. I'll sue their ass off."

Willow laughed. "It's you," she said. "You're back." She pushed to her feet, the baby making her heavy, absurd. The barred sides were up on the bed. She yearned to bend and hug the skeletal figure under the sheet and pale blanket. But bending was a problem these days anyway. She reached out across the barrier, half laughing, half crying. "Oh, God, Mabel. It's been so long. I ached with missing you. I came and sat with you, and you didn't even know it. And when they phoned today, I thought for sure you were dead."

"Hell," Mabel said, "it would take more than a bullet to finish me." She pawed awkwardly at the pillows under her head, found something, held it up for Willow to take. Willow took it—a little, misshapen lump of lead. Mabel said, "When I hit the floor, it fell out. Can you beat that? Just fell out. The jigs didn't notice—not them. They didn't even tumble to what'd happened when I told them my God damn arm was broken. A patient who hadn't said a word in a year and a half. Willow, a dog is smarter than that."

"But doctors came from all over." Willow peered at the horrible pebble in her palm. "They said if they tried to take it out, it would kill you."

Mabel snorted. "What did I always tell you about doctors? You think they learn medicine with all that expensive education? What they learn is how to take your money." She barked a laugh. "You should have seen them milling around my room. One of the ass-holes said it was a miracle. No kidding. A miracle, he said. Then the orderly sweeping up under my bed put the bullet in his hand. Hah. You should have seen the expression on his face." She reached up. "Give it to me. I'm going to put it on a chain and wear it around my neck. To remind me to get along without a little help from my friends. Did you read what Berger said about my script? Jew bastard."

"When are they going to let you come home?" Willow said.

"They have to feed me up, exercise me to get

the muscle tone back, all that crap. I don't know. They—" She stopped, scowling. "What the hell happened to you? Are you fat? You didn't get fat on me, did you?" This time she managed to push herself to an almost-sitting position, struggling, wincing. "For Christ sake. Do I see what I think I see? Open those fucking curtains."

"The light will make your head ache," Willow said numbly.

"Not like you make my head ache," Mabel said. "I can't believe this. I just can't. I always knew you were a hopeless jerk, but one thing I never thought was that I had to warn you where babies come from. Who did it? That slick little shyster, right? Nash? 'Tennis, anyone?' "

"Mabel, stop. You don't understand."

Mabel laughed sourly, scrounged down in the bed, turned her back to Willow. "I wasn't out of the way long, was I? Jesus, I remember all those heart to heart talks we had. What we both felt about men. We were soul-mates, right? You and me against the world."

"It was true," Willow cried. "It still is."

"They named you right," Mabel said. "Bend with the wind. That's how willows survive. Never a broken twig."

"Mabel." Willow drew breath, made her voice steady. "You mentioned doctors and money. Do you have any idea how much it costs to keep a comatose patient under constant monitoring for sixteen months in a hospital?"

"Costs?" Mabel rolled over sharply to squint through the shadows, angry, scornful. "What in hell are you talking about? I didn't have a dime to my name. Patients like me don't cost anything. Dear God, Willow! What are you going to tell me now—that you didn't know about Medicare?"

"You wouldn't have been looked after the way they've done here. You'd have died, Mabel—just died."

"Bullshit," Mabel said, and turned her back again.

"I couldn't let that happen," Willow said.

"I can see what you could let happen," Mabel said bitterly. "Let the first man who ever asked you stick his cock into you. Disgusting. Clear out, will you, and leave me alone? A little decency, okay?"

Willow clenched her fists. "Mabel, I did it for you."

Mabel snorted. "You better get yourself a writer. That's the corniest dialog I ever heard. Will you clear out now, please? I'm weak. I have to sleep."

Willow rattled the bed bars. Her eyes stung with furious tears. "You've slept for months. Mabel, I tried to pay it off. I took a job. You remember Emil at the Hungry Hungarian? He let me be a waitress. It wasn't enough."

"And me without my violin," Mabel said. "You are one empty-headed fool. You always were, but I thought at least you loved me, and we were going to stick together, no matter what. Willow, the government pays for sick people when they don't have the money." She mocked Willow's voice: " 'Mabel, I tried to pay it off.' God have mercy. Nurse!" She groped with her good arm until she caught the dangling switch to summon help. "Nurse!" she bellowed. "Is there a God damn nurse on this floor who isn't out to lunch?"

"Nash paid for all of this," Willow said. "I couldn't let him. That money in my father's will."

"Nurse!" Mabel shouted.

"I had to get that. There was no other way."

"What's the problem?" It wasn't a nurse who came. It was Ellen McMahon, in her intern's whites again. Willow hadn't seen her in many weeks. She looked Willow up and down, frowned, stepped to the bed, where Mabel continued to roar. "Miss Stoner," Ellen McMahon said, "calm down, or I'll have to give you a shot."

"Get the brood mare out of here," Mabel said.

The doctor turned to Willow with an apologetic shrug of shoulders and eyebrows. "Excitement's counter-indicated," she said. "Why not come back tomorrow?"

"I won't be receiving," Mabel said.

"I have to explain," Willow said. But the doctor's hand was in the small of her back, where the perpetual ache lay, and Willow was being pushed out of the room into the cramped, lowceilinged, cluttered hallway. The door fell shut behind her. "Excuse me," the doctor said, and hurried away. Willow stared at the closed door, too stunned for tears, too stunned for any feeling at all. "There's so much to explain," she said, but no one heard her.

For a complete list of books available from Penguin in the United States, write to Dept. DG, Penguin Books, 299 Murray Hill Parkway, East Rutherford, New Jersey 07073.

For a complete list of books available from Penguin in Canada, write to Penguin Books Canada Limited, 2801 John Street, Markham, Ontario L3R 1B4.